1

The big concord stage swayed over the rutted road, the crude springs doing little to ease the continuous jolting of the passengers inside. The six horses, urged by the skilful wielding of the lash and the vituperation of the driver, settled themselves for the uphill pull on the last stage of their journey. On the box the driver, handling reins and whip as well as he managed the outsized plug of tobacco in his cheek, spat a brown stream into the dust and grinned at the man beside him.

'Reckon you can relax now, Jud. Another mile and we'll be at the post station.'

'None too soon for me.' The guard wiped his mouth with the back of his hand and settled his shotgun more comfortably in the crook of his arm. He, like the driver, wore a Colt, strapped

1

around his waist, his belt studded with cartridges. A bandolier of shotgun ammunition hung around his chest and another containing ammunition for the Winchester in the seat-scabbard crossed it just below the open neck of the man's shirt. Automatically he turned his head, staring backwards down the winding trail and then glancing to either side. He was watching for enemies, red or white, who would be only too willing to attack the stage for the sake of the cash carried by the passengers, the mail-box in the boot or merely for the sake of taking revenge against the hated white man.

He saw nothing and relaxed as the lead horses pulled the stage up the incline on the top of which the post station offered the safety of a wooden stockade, a change of horses and a hot meal. Dust swirled from the wheels as the driver tugged at the reins and the guard, as usual, lifted his gun from his belt and triggered three shots in quick sequence. A man ran from the log-house, stared towards the stage and

THE FIRST SHOT

Six years earlier the Circle Bar had been thriving, but now Rex Willard saw an impoverished ranch, his brother missing and his father a hopeless drunk. And there were enemies all around: ruthless cattle barons and Daren, the killer foreman of the Flying W. Could Rex win back his inheritance, and find his missing brother? Against the odds, but helped by his friends, he just might achieve justice. But whatever the outcome, death would stalk the range.

E. C. TUBB

THE FIRST SHOT

Complete and Unabridged

LINFORD
Leicester

First published in Great Britain in 2000

Originally published in paperback as
Colt Vengeance by James R. Fenner.

First Linford Edition
published 2006

The moral right of the author has been asserted

British Library CIP Data

Tubb, E. C.
    The first shot.—Large print ed.—
Linford western library
    1. Western stories 2. Large type books
    I. Title II. Fenner, James R. Colt vengeance
823.9'14 [F]

ISBN 1–84617–475–9

Published by
F. A. Thorpe (Publishing)
Anstey, Leicestershire

Set by Words & Graphics Ltd.
Anstey, Leicestershire
Printed and bound in Great Britain by
T. J. International Ltd., Padstow, Cornwall

This book is printed on acid-free paper

immediately began to beat on an iron triangle. Dust rose then settled as the driver slammed on his brakes.

'Made it with two minutes to spare.' He wiped the dust from a thick watch, glanced at it, nodded and tucked it back into its leather-lined pocket. 'And let that McHenry try to tell me different. This is one stage that always gets through on time.'

'Hold your fire, Bill.' The guard lifted his rifle and tossed it down into the eager hands of a gangling youngster who had run from the house to meet the stage. He followed it with the shotgun and then climbed stiffly down from his high perch.

'All out folks!' The driver jerked open the door of the stage. 'We eat here. One hour stay so do what you got to do and make it fast.'

Five men stepped from the stage. Two were miners, bearded, dressed in thick flannel shirts and knee-boots, their leather jackets stained and torn, the guns at their waist worn more

3

because of custom than for any other purpose. Indians rarely attacked the gold diggings and on their sprees in town they relied on their fists and heavy boots to settle arguments. They headed immediately for the log-house and the food which would be waiting on the tables.

A preacher followed them, dressed in dark broadcloth, unarmed, his face wrinkled and his eyes kind. He paused to stretch himself and then followed the miners. A gambler came next, fashionably dressed in high boots, cutaway coat, embroidered waistcoat and half-plug hat. He wore gloves and his face was pale as if shielded from strong sunlight. He coughed as he stepped from the stage, holding on to the door until the attack passed, dabbing at his lips with a white handkerchief. When he finally straightened the handkerchief was flecked with blood.

'Cough troubling you, Dancer?' The remaining occupant of the stage had waited patiently until the gambler had mastered his attack. He was tall, lean, his blue eyes seeming even brighter from reason of his sunburned face. He wore store clothes and carried a bag. Unlike the gambler he carried a pair of Colts at his waist, the twin butts almost concealed by his coat. He tipped back his wide brimmed hat and stared at the station.

'I'm all right, Rex.' The gambler smiled. 'Nothing to worry about.'

'Of course not.' Rex Willard took a deep breath of the sage-scented air. 'You'll soon recover in this country. I told you that the air was as good as medicine.'

'You folks want to eat?' a broad, red-faced man yelled to them from the open door of the house. He was McHenry, the factor of the station and self-appointed cook. His job was to provide the food the passengers needed when the stage halted at his station. As the price of the food was included in the fare most passengers grumbled at its quality, its quantity or both.

Rex nodded and led the way towards the house. Behind him the gangling youngster wrestled with the horses, leading the jaded ones to their stable and harnessing the fresh team. The old team would be fed, rested, rubbed down and be ready for the next stage. An oldster, sitting in the sun, spat and called out ribald advice to the youth. The youngster ignored it but, as if by accident, the rearing team lunged towards the old man making him skip out of the way. McHenry, aware of the byplay, cursed and shook his fist.

'Darn fool,' he muttered as he led the way into the house. 'Tricks like that can cause trouble. A kick from a horse ain't anything to laugh about.'

'Depends on who gets the kick,' said Rex evenly. 'Me, I remember one time when some Yankees was trying to shod their horses a sergeant got himself kicked in a delicate place. He couldn't sit easy for a week. We all reckoned it the funniest thing we ever saw.'

'You fight for the Union?' McHenry

didn't say more than that but his expression conveyed his feelings. The tall man shook his head.

'Not exactly. I was taken prisoner by them and set to digging earthworks. Guess they were some of the poorest defences a man ever did see.'

'You was with the South then?' McHenry smiled. 'I know the war's over but I'd sure hate to have to feed a man who was on the wrong side.' He gestured towards the table. 'Better dive in, folks, them miners sure can put away the victuals.'

The food was rough but wholesome. Beans, pork, corn bread and plenty of hot, strong coffee. Rex ate like a man who knows the value of food, emulating the miners in his concentration on the food. Dancer, after toying with his fork, finally dropped all pretence at eating and, lighting a long, black cigar, leaned back sipping his coffee. The preacher ate slowly but with a grim determination. His slowness was caused by his ill-fitting false teeth, his determination from the fact that he didn't know where his next meal was coming from.

'Seen anything on the trip, Bill?' McHenry belched and stared at the driver. He always made a point of eating with the passengers as if to prove the quality of his cooking. Bill shook his head.

'Nary a sign. Don't really expect it this close to town. No Indians anyways.'

'They got the Eastbound stage last week,' said McHenry. 'Sam found it gutted and the passengers minus their hair. Got the driver and shotgun too. Apaches.' He spat thoughtfully on the sanded floor. 'Guess a bunch of braves broke out of the reservation again.'

'Guess so.' Bill slowly cut a fresh plug and loaded his cheek. 'Maybe one day them smart soldiers will do something to protect the stages. All they seem to do now is to wander around impressing the girls with their fancy uniforms.'

'I'll teach them how Indians should be handled.' Jud patted his shotgun. 'What them Bucks need is a load of buckshot.' He laughed at his own humour. 'Get it? Buckshot for the Bucks.'

'Some horses need a tight bit,' said Bill acidly. 'You fire jokes like that at the Indians and you won't be needing no shotgun. They'll be too scared to come back for more ever to bother us again.' He spat a thin stream of brown juice. 'Buckshot for Bucks,' he muttered. 'You want people to think you've been kicked on the head by a mule?'

'Jud don't mean no harm,' soothed McHenry. He changed the subject. 'You bring me anything this trip?'

'Him,' Bill jerked a thumb towards Rex. 'A couple of boxes of shells and a gross of horseshoe nails.'

'No chewing tobacco?' McHenry looked hurt. 'Hell, Bill, you know I asked special for some molasses pressed plug.'

'I ain't forgotten. I'll drop it off on the way back. No sense in carrying that stull all the way here when you've got a town not more than fifty miles away. I'll pick it up in Lamonte.' He tugged out his watch and glanced at it. 'Ten minutes, folks, and then we roll.'

The miners burped and hastily left the table, going outside on their private business. The preacher cleaned his plate and reached for his coffee. Rex accepted a cigar from the gambler, lit it, and stared through the smoke.

'Sure you won't change your mind?'

'I'm no cowpuncher, Rex. From what I hear there are enough saloons in Lamonte to keep me busy. I'll buy a concession or operate on percentage until I can figure things out. I'll get by.'

'I hope so. You know where I'm to be found if you need me. Just send word down to the Circle Bar. Twin Forks is the town, everyone knows the brand.'

'I'll remember it.' Dancer hesitated. 'You know where to come if you want a straight game.'

'I'm finished with gambling.' Rex stared at the tip of his cigar. 'I reckon that I've done enough of that during the past six years, taken plenty of chances too.'

'Six years?'

'Sure.' Rex shrugged. 'You may as well know. My father owns the spread and me and my brother operated it with him. There was a girl, never mind about that, she chose Mark, my brother. I didn't want to stick around so I rode off. Then the war came along. You know the rest.'

'Enlisted, captured, prisoner of war for two years.' Dancer nodded. 'I know.'

'You should, we were together for all of those two years.' Rex's face hardened as he thought about it. 'It was a tough time, Dancer, but it's over now. From now on I'm going to live a peaceful life. Riding the range, round-up, driving the beef to market, that's what I want to do.'

'And your brother?'

'War makes a man grow up fast, Dancer. I've rid myself of that foolishness. Nancy made her choice, well, that's over now. Dad was old when I left and won't be any younger. He can do with all the help he can get and I reckon that I owe it to him to do what I can.'

'Glad to hear it.' Dancer coughed again, bending almost double as he fought to control the spasms which tore at his lungs. The preacher stared at him with mournful eyes, waiting until the gambler had controlled himself before speaking.

'Lung-fever, young sir?'

'I guess so.'

'A man suffering from that should turn his thoughts to higher things,' droned the old man. 'I see by your clothing that you are a man who places much value on the mundane things instead of lifting your heart and looking higher. I — '

'Just a minute, preacher.' Rex leaned forward. He had recognized the man for what he was, one of the group of itinerant preachers who moved from place to place preaching where they could. They belonged to no regular church and many of them were outright opportunists. Some of them were sincere, carrying a little light and gentleness into the violence of the frontier towns. 'I know you mean well,' he said, 'but my friend is ill. Are you staying in Lamonte?'

'That is my hope and intention.'

'Good.' Gold gleamed as Rex slipped a coin into the man's hand. 'I'd take it kindly if you would find a doctor when you arrive, and have him look at my friend. I know that I can rely on you.'

'I don't need his help, Rex.' Dancer was angry. 'I can look after myself.'

'I know.' Rex smiled towards the figure of the preacher as he left the room. 'But you're careless and forgetful, Dancer, sometimes too careless and forgetful. You know what that prison camp doctor told you.'

'Take things easy. Head West to get the clean air. No smoking or drinking or late nights. No nothing.' The gambler snorted. 'He might as well have nailed me down while he was at it.'

'He was giving you the straight information. If that preacher can make you see a doctor then I'll be happy.' Rex grinned. 'And he'll be happy too. That type of man has to be helping someone else or stay miserable. You want him to be miserable?'

Dancer seemed about to protest, changed his mind and shrugged. 'Have it your way, Rex. I'm in no mind to argue with the man who saved my life. Not now. Maybe later but not now.'

'Time, folks.' Bill glanced at his watch for the last time. 'Get aboard or get left. We're rolling.'

Rex followed the gambler out to the stage. The miners and the preacher had already climbed aboard. Jud, the guard, examined his weapons and mounted to the box. The driver whistled, cracked his whip and yelled at the team as they settled in their collars. With a cloud of dust the stage rolled from the compound and out on to the trail. Rex stood watching it as it dwindled into the distance.

'Bill's a good driver,' said McHenry. 'He'll make the other station afore dark and Lamonte by sundown tomorrow. That is if nothing happens to him on the way.'

'Indians pretty bad in these parts?'

'So so. I ain't complaining. They tried to raid us once but we beat them off. Mostly they swoop down from the hills on the stages or maybe attack some homesteads.' McHenry sucked at his teeth.

''Course, if things get worse I don't know what will happen. So far the Apaches have been kept pretty close to the treaty. But if the rumours I hear are true then all hell's liable to break out soon.'

'How?'

'They're cutting into their land, the Indian land I mean. The agent is a tight-wad who aims to get rich at the expense of the Indians. Maybe some Indians will stand for that treatment but not the Apache. Soon as they get hungry they'll come down and start raiding again. Winter'll be the time and if they ain't fed then they'll start mixing warpaint and sharpening their knives.'

The factor shrugged as if shaking off an unpleasant thought. 'Well, mister, what can I do for you?'

'I want a horse, a good one. Some food and a rifle if you have it.'

'I've got it.'

'Let's see them.'

The horse was a roan gelding, a big, strong, fast looking animal with a deep chest and fine withers. Rex examined the animal, looking at its teeth and running his hand down the insides of its legs in search of galls or sores. He found none.

'I take care of my horses,' said McHenry. 'That beast will carry you until it bursts its heart. Cow-trained too. A bargain at forty dollars.'

'Where's the saddle?'

'You want that too?'

'Sure, you think I can ride bare-backed?' Rex waited as a saddle was brought out for his inspection. He nodded and checked the rifle suspended in the scabbard. It was a Winchester, almost new and nicely balanced. He took a couple of trial shots, sending the second bullet directly on top of the first. McHenry whistled.

'You can shoot anyway.'

'I had time to learn.' Rex looked at the factor. 'How much, inclusive?'

'With a warbag of flour and belly pork say,' the factor screwed up his eyes as if in deep mental computation.

'Say a hundred and fifty dollars.'

'Say a hundred and ten,' suggested Rex.

'I ain't a man to haggle,' said the factor. 'A hundred and forty and the stuff's yours.'

They settled for a hundred and thirty. Rex counted out the money while the factor wrote out his bill of sale for the horse. He had a little trouble over the brand.

'Guess it must be Double X,' he said. 'Whoever did it must have had a shaky hand.'

'Did you buy the horse?'

'No. Fella traded it in a couple of months ago for a ticket on the stage. He had a bill of sale so I didn't argue.'

He looked at Rex. 'It's all right,' he assured. 'I'm known in these parts and there'll be no trouble. Any complaints you refer them to me. I wouldn't buy a horse from no Indian or Mex and even from a white man I've got to know him or see a bill of sale.' He rummaged in a drawer of his desk. 'See, here's the original. The brand is Double X at that, guess they must have used a cold iron.'

Rex hesitated then closed the bargain. He was wise enough in the ways of the West to know that a man riding a horse for which he had no bill of sale was liable to run into trouble. Horse stealing was one of the most heinous crimes of the frontier and punished by a length of rope thrown over the nearest tree. It was crude justice but essential. A man could lose his life through the loss of his horse. But he had a bill of sale, the factor was a responsible man or he wouldn't have been in charge of the station and he felt satisfied.

And he was going home to people who knew him well.

2

The Circle Bar lay on the foothills of the Apache Mountains between the Pecos and the Rio Grande. Old man Willard had come into the country with the first wave of settlers back in 1840. Rex, then scarcely able to stand, didn't remember much of their life previous to the trek and had grown up on the range. Mark, his brother, had been born on the ranch; Fred, his uncle, had died there during an Indian attack, and his rough wooden grave marker stood along with that of his sister, his cousin and two hired hands, all of whom had died defending the outpost of civilization.

Rex thought of these things as he rode easily from the stage station, heading south towards the land he knew so well. He took his time, halting when the sun slid beneath the horizon and building himself a camp fire and cooking sourdough cakes from the flour in his warbag, boiling coffee and smoking a cigar before rolling in his blankets.

The emptiness of the prairie, the soft scent of sun-dried sage and the thin, distant singing of the coyotes brought a strange peace. For six years he had wandered from the land where he had been raised, four of them spent in the turmoil of war. Now he wanted nothing but to be allowed to take up life where he had left it, to rise at dawn, to ride the herds, to take some of the burden of running the ranch from the shoulders of his ageing father.

On the third day he saw the buzzards. They wheeled and circled high in the clear air, tiny black dots against the heavens, waiting, Rex knew, for someone or some animal to die. Unconsciously he spurred his mount to greater speed, guiding it to the spot around which the buzzards wheeled. It could be no more than a coyote or a buffalo strayed far from the herds to the north. It could be a horse or a lost calf. Or it could be a man.

It was neither.

A small fire lay amid trampled grass, the ashes barely cold. A calf lay to one side, its foreleg twisted and its great eyes reflecting its terror. Rex slid from his saddle, looked at the injured beast and his right hand Colt sounded once as he drove a merciful bullet into its brain. Frowning, he stared about him, his nostrils wrinkled to a barely detected odour. It was familiar, that smell, the scent of burned hair and scorched hide produced when hot branding irons were touched to the heaving flanks of calves and mavericks. Someone had been doing some branding and had been careless about their work. They had left in a hurry too, the calf had been injured when roped and the roper, whoever he was, had not shot the injured beast.

Normal cowpunchers would never have left the animal in pain. Normal cowpunchers would not have ridden off at the approach of a stranger. Normal cowpunchers wouldn't have been branding now anyway, that was done only twice a year during round up. The signs pointed clearly to the fact that someone had been doing some illegal branding.

Rex tipped his hat back on his head and stooped to examine the prints of horses. The ground was hard but he could tell that there had been at least three mounts. He straightened just in time to see a group of horsemen galloping towards him.

There were five of them, led by a red-faced man who sported silver-decorated belts, chaps and saddle. He pulled up with a jerk of his reins, stared about him and swore.

'They've been at it again! Daren! Come over here.'

'What is it, Clive?' Daren, a very dried-up cowpuncher, nudged his horse forward and leaned over his saddle. He stared about him, sucked at his teeth then looked at Rex. 'Well, want to say anything?'

'What am I supposed to say?' Rex stared from one to the other. 'I got here a mite before you did. I saw what you can see.'

'Rustlers!' Clive seemed burning with anger. 'All the time it's rustlers.'

'Maybe we've caught one this time.' Daren stared at Rex with pale, hard eyes. 'Seems strange to me that a stranger should be here just at this time. When did you say you got here?'

'Just before you did.'

'See anyone?'

'No. My guess is that they spotted me and rode off.'

Daren nodded and swung from his saddle. He felt the ashes of the fire, blew on them and they flamed red. He looked at the calf then, before Rex could guess his intention, had turned, the Colt in his hand pointing at the tall man's stomach.

'You just got here, you said.' His lips thinned over his teeth. 'You saw no one at all. Yet the fire's still hot and that calf is still bleeding.' The hammer clicked on his gun as he thumbed it to full cock. 'Better start explaining, mister.'

'I shot the calf.' Rex forced his muscles to relax. 'The rest is as I told you.'

'Maybe.' Daren didn't holster his gun. 'Or maybe we arrived a mite too soon. Seems to me that a man would say what you've said if he was caught running a hot iron.'

'I haven't got an iron.' Rex shrugged. He had no real right to be angry, that he knew. Rustling, along with horse stealing, was a crime usually punished by a quick hanging. In Daren's place he would probably have done the same. Strangers, in the West, were objects of suspicion until they had proved themselves. With the ranches spread all over the ranges, with thousands of cattle controlled by only a handful of men, it was too easy for rustlers to operate, cutting out a few head and shipping them over the river for a quick sale in Mexico.

'Look,' said Rex. 'I know how you

feel but I'm telling the truth. Check my gear if you want, you won't find either rope or iron. Can't see how a man can rope and brand without either.'

'He's talking sense,' said one of the other riders.

'You shut your mouth, Benson.' Daren didn't look at the speaker. 'I'll handle this.'

'Then how about doing something other than stand there with a gun in your hand?' Rex glanced at Clive. 'You the boss?'

'I'm Clive Leyburn, boss of the Flying W. Daren's my ramrod.' He spoke over his shoulder. 'Check his gear, Benson.'

'And the gun?'

'The gun stays.'

Rex sighed and waited for Benson to clear him. Opposite, a few yards away, Daren still held his Colt levelled on his stomach. Rex began to dislike the foreman intensely, he had seen the expression in the pale, hard eyes before. Daren was a killer, a man who would rather shoot than argue, a man who had grown trigger-happy and inflated with his own importance.

'Hey, Boss!' Benson sounded excited. 'Look at this!'

'You find a rope or iron?'

'No, but look at this horse.' Benson led the animal forward. 'Recognize it?'

'I think — ' Clive frowned at the mount. Suddenly he swung from his saddle and ran his hand over the flank, staring at the brand.

'It's the roan that was stolen three months ago.' Benson pointed at the brand. 'See that? Someone overburned the W and tried to make it into a double X.'

'You're right.' Clive turned, his own Colt in his hand. 'All right, mister,' he said. 'Start talking.'

'Take it easy,' Rex glanced at the circle of faces. They were, if anything, harder than before, 'Mind if I smoke?' Without waiting for permission he took a cigar from his pocket, lit it and threw the match into the ashes of the fire.

'One thing at a time. Do you still think I'm a rustler?'

'No rope or iron,' said Benson quickly. 'Can't see how he could be.'

'He could have ridden with those that did have rope and iron,' pointed out Clive.

'Then why didn't I ride off with them?' Rex slowly drew at his cigar. 'Now as for the horse. I bought it a few days ago at the stage station from the factor, McHenry. I've got his bill of sale in my pocket.'

'Bills of sale can be forged,' said Daren. He licked his lips with nervous anticipation.

'I know that.' Rex gestured with his cigar. 'But this one isn't. You can ride up to the station if you like and check. McHenry showed me the original from the man he took the horse from.'

'That's my horse,' said Clive. 'It was stolen from me about three months ago.'

'I've only your word for that,' said Rex quietly.

'The brand's been changed.'

'Maybe not. It could be an original Double X brand.'

'I know my own horses.' Clive was beginning to lose his temper. 'Are you trying to call me a liar?'

'Are you me?'

'If you say that horse isn't mine then you're a liar.'

'You've got four men with you,' said Rex evenly. 'And you've got a gun in your hand. Seems to me that it don't take much courage for a man to talk big in those circumstances.'

'I'd talk the same anyway.'

'Maybe, but how about proving it?'

'Pay no attention to him, Clive.' Daren looked ugly. 'For my money he's a horse-stealing rustler and should be treated as such. I say let's shoot him and get it over.'

'You'd be killing an innocent man.' Rex looked at Clive. 'All right, so maybe it was your horse, but I didn't steal it. If you don't believe me then you can believe McHenry. And I've got other proof too. Three months ago I wasn't anywhere near this country. I couldn't have stolen your horse.'

'Kill him,' said Daren.

'Take it easy.' Benson eased himself in his saddle. 'I'd be the first to plug him if he was guilty but you've got to give him a chance. We ain't murdering Indians to cut down everyone we see. Give him a chance.'

'I told you once,' said Daren savagely. 'I don't aim to tell you again. You shut your mouth, Benson, and keep it shut.'

'I get forty dollars a month and bed and board,' said the cowpuncher. 'For that I'll work twenty-four hours a day. I'll freeze in winter and roast in summer. I'll fight Indians, rustlers and horse-thieves. I'll be shot at and kill if I have to. But that forty a month don't pay me for taking that sort of talk from a ramrod.'

'You'll take it and like it.'

'I won't take it and I won't have to like it.' Benson swung down from his saddle. 'Put up your iron and we'll see how good you talk without it.'

'Benson!' Clive stepped in front of the man. 'You going out of your mind?'

'So Daren reckons he's good with a gun.' Benson shrugged. 'Maybe he is, maybe he ain't. I aim to find out just how good he is.'

'Let him go, Clive.' Daren licked his lips. 'Stand back and give him his chance.' Slowly he released the hammer of his gun, uncocking it and slipping it into its holster. 'Ready, Benson?'

'Daren! I'm telling you to quit this nonsense.' Clive glared at his foreman. 'You shoot Benson and you're through with the Flying W.'

'That'll make two of us,' said the foreman. 'Me and Benson both.' He glared at the cowpuncher, his body falling into a crouch, his hand hovering over the butt of his gun. 'All right, you,' he gritted. 'You've talked big. Now reach for your iron or eat dirt.'

Clive stared at him, recognized that nothing he could do or say would make any difference. And there was nothing he could do or say. He was boss but that was all. If two men wanted to shoot it out he couldn't stop them and would be a fool if he did. Interference with personal quarrels would not be tolerated by the men he hired to work for him. He scowled and bit his lips as Benson moved forward.

The cowpuncher was a short, thick-set man with calm eyes and an untroubled expression. Within the next few seconds, as far as he knew, he would kill or be killed depending on the speed of his draw and the accuracy of his aim. Like Daren he crouched so as to give his hand free play towards the butt of the Colt in its tied-down holster. Watching, Rex knew that the man didn't stand a chance.

He glanced to either side of him. Everyone was concentrating on the two men. He moved his hands, letting them fall to the twin guns at his waist. No one saw the motion. Abruptly he whipped out the Colts, thumbed back the hammers and fired two shots into the air.

'Hold it!'

Daren swore, startled by the explosions and turned, his gun swinging level. Rex fired, his bullet striking the sidegate on the foreman's pistol and tearing it from his hand. His other gun menaced Benson.

'Take it easy. Put up your gun!'

Benson stared at the tall man, at the twin Colts and determined expression. Slowly he returned his gun to its holster. Daren, nursing his numbed wrist, swore with helpless anger.

'Damn rustler! I said we should kill him.'

'Shut your mouth.' Rex looked at Clive. 'You're the boss and where I come from a boss is someone who can give orders and make them stick. You that kind of a boss?'

'I think so.'

'Then give orders that no one's to pull a gun. Understood?'

'No.' Clive was frank. 'What you after?'

'I aim to clear up this mess. I could

do it the hard way. I could make you drop your guns and start walking and when you'd gone, ride on slowly and easy. Maybe if I was just passing through that's what I'd do. But I prefer the other way. You called me a rustler and horse thief. All right. I aim to make you eat them words. But I can't do it when fools like your ramrod want to perforate me before I can speak.' He nodded towards the foreman. 'Seems to me a man so eager to get shooting is maybe a man who wants something hidden.'

'That's crazy talk,' said Clive. 'Daren's been with me for most of five years now.'

'You started the Flying W around that time?'

'That's about it. Why, what's it to you?'

'Ever heard of the Circle Bar?'

'I've heard of it.' Clive was grim. 'Too damn much of it.'

Rex glanced sharply at the boss of the Flying W. There had been hate in the man's voice when he spoke of the other ranch. He hefted the Colts in his hands.

'Better give that order,' he said quietly. 'No shooting. If you don't someone's liable to get themselves hurt real bad.'

'Meaning me?'

'Could be.'

For a long moment Clive stared at Rex then snapped his orders.

'No shooting. Any man that pulls a gun will have me to deal with. That goes for you, too, Daren.' He waited as Rex holstered his guns. 'Now what?'

'Now we get down to business.' Rex took the bill of sale from his pocket. 'First you can look at this. It's genuine.' He held out another paper. 'Military discharge from the Confederacy. I was released three months ago, the time you reckon your horse was stolen. Maybe you'd like to tell me how I could be a thousand miles east and here at the same time.'

Clive stared at the papers. He was breathing hard and when he looked up his eyes glittered with anger.

'Rex Willard. Is that you?'

'That's me.'

'I might have guessed it.' Clive flung back the papers, Rex caught them, folded them and tucked them back in his pocket.

'Seems you've no love for the name,' he said 'Maybe you've got your reasons?'

'I don't have to waste words on you!' Rex saw that the boss of the Flying W was quivering with rage. 'I've warned the Circle Bar to stay off my land. That goes for everyone who owns it and who rides for it.'

'Hold it.' Rex felt his own temper rising. 'Seems that as we're to be neighbours that's no way to talk. I didn't come home aiming to start a feud.'

'You've walked into one, boy.' Benson had remounted his horse and now called down from the saddle: 'Best you can do is to get home as fast as you can.'

'That was my intention.' Rex reached

for his horse then spun as Clive jerked at his shoulder.

'That's my horse.'

'I figure different.' Rex stared at the circle of faces then back at Leyburn. 'What is this? You trying to steal my horse?'

'Your horse!' Abruptly the red-faced man lashed out with his fist. Rex, caught off balance, staggered back against the roan, which reared and struck out with its hoofs. Clive Leyburn sprang forward, his fists smashing at the tall man's face and body. Rex grunted as blows drove the breath from his lungs and sent the taste of blood into his mouth. Savagely he regained his balance and leapt to the attack.

Leyburn was a big man, solid, his body packed with muscle. Rex was but a few months from the prison hospital, still weak after his confinement and half-dazed by the sudden attack. Even so he stood his ground, making up for his weakness by a calculated attack, swaying to avoid the hammer-blows of the other man, sending his own fists against eyes and nose and mouth. Leyburn, his face streaming blood, staggered back as Rex slammed his right into his stomach.

'Kill him!' It was Daren. 'Give him the boot.'

Maddened with the pain of his injuries, Leyburn rushed forward. Agony lanced through Rex as a swinging fist drove against his heart. Desperately he dodged a knee thrust towards his groin, feeling his thigh go numb as it took the force of the blow. Nails tore his cheeks as fingers reached for his eyes. The smell of blood and dust rose around him, mingled with the animal odour of sweat. The sound of panting breath echoed in his ears and Leyburn, his teeth bared in a snarl of hatred, seemed to be wavering in the midst of a fog.

Then Rex forgot to fight like a civilized man.

It was pain that did it, pain and fury aroused by the unfairness of what had happened. He had tried to be fair and understanding and they had treated him with contempt and brutality. The time for gentleness had passed. Leyburn would beat him into a pulp unless he could get the upper hand.

There is a state of mind essential to any fighter who hopes to win. Thought has no place in it, nor contempt, nor reckoning of the consequences. Rex had tried to fight with his mind, pulling his punches a little and obeying the vague rules of combat. Now he threw everything aside and concentrated on but one thought, to win and win quickly.

He didn't feel the fists which smashed against him. He felt none of the pain from the blows. Instead he began to fight with fists and boots, knees and elbows, smashing again at the red face of his opponent, swinging his elbow and using his boots and knees. A redness seemed to fill his mind and only dimly was he aware of distant shouting.

'Stop it! Stop it before you kill him!'

Benson jerked at his arm, pulling him away from the limp figure on the ground.

'Get away from me.' Rex flung the cowpuncher aside.

'Get hold of yourself.' Benson stared warily at the tall man. 'Quit now or I'll buffalo you.'

'I'll handle this.' Daren strode forward, his gun in his hand. Rex recognized the threat, tried to go for his guns then staggered as a lariat fell over his shoulders, tightening with a jerk and trapping his arms to his sides.

'Your sort ain't wanted around here,' snarled the foreman. 'Neither you, your old man or that no-good brother of yours. We've told them what to expect if they're found on Flying W territory and now I'm telling you. As far as we're concerned it's open season on the Circle Bar.'

Rex spat in his face.

'You'll pay for that,' said the foreman. 'I'll gut-shoot you and leave you screaming.'

'Not now,' said Benson sharply. 'You

heard what the boss said. No shooting.'

'I heard.' Daren uncocked his gun. 'It'll keep. But just to remind you — ' The gun lashed out and struck Rex's cheek, laying open the flesh to the bone. 'And just to remind you that your breed ain't wanted in these parts — '

He yelled and the man holding the lariat struck spurs into his horse. The rope tightened as the animal bounded away dragging Rex behind it. Bound, helpless to save himself, he rolled and bounced over the prairie. The rider yelped as he rode in a circle halting close to the ashes of the fire.

'Now remember, Willard.' Daren stared down at the helpless man. 'You're not wanted here. Get out of this territory and stay out.'

Rex struggled to rise. He was bruised, aching, his head spinning and his mouth filled with blood. Despite that he managed to stagger to his feet. Swaying, he stared at the foreman.

'You'd better kill me,' he said thickly. 'You'd better do it now while you've got the chance. Because if you don't then I'm going to kill you. I'll do it if it's the last thing I do.'

Daren laughed and sunlight flashed from the barrel of his Colt as he lifted it above Rex's head. Viciously he swung the three-pound weapon, the long barrel catching the tall man just above the ear. Buffaloed, Rex crumpled without a sound.

High above, wheeling in the air, the buzzards circled. Waiting.

3

Sam Dancer was a gambler both by profession and inclination. Before the war he had operated on the riverboats, dealing cards to those who travelled the Mississippi from New Orleans to St. Louis, making a small fortune from the wealthy cotton dealers, slave traders and manufacturers from the industrial north. The war had caught him at a disadvantage: his intelligence told him that the agricultural south could never win, his weakness for a gamble had made him take the long chance.

He had lost as so many others had lost. He had been wounded, flung into a prison hospital and forced to live in conditions which had killed many and weakened many more. Now, his lungs ruined, he had headed West to spend what was left of his life. Rex, the only man he regarded as a friend, had left him to ride down to his ranch. Dancer had wasted little time in finding a place for himself in Lamonte.

It wasn't hard to do. In these times, professional gamblers were respected members of the community, the games they ran an accepted part of the social structure. True, there were cheats and tinhorns, bottom-dealers and card-sharps, but most of them were soon recognized and either run out of town on a rail or, if they argued about it, planted in boot hill. A straight dealer was accepted as being a man who was willing to stake all he owned against all comers. With poker the main recreation such a man could swiftly build himself a stake — provided that he didn't ruin himself by tangling with better players.

Dancer looked over town, chose the second largest saloon and demanded to see the owner. Mike Killigan had originally come from the Emerald Isle and had a cheerful, good-natured face, a hard hand and a shrewd business sense.

'I don't hold with sharp dealing at all,' he said. 'What's the good of killing the goose is what I say. If it's a proposition you'll be having in mind then maybe you'd better be telling me.'

'You can let me run a table for you, pay me keep and a cut of the profits, or you can let me operate on my own.' Dancer brushed a speck of dust from his lapel. 'In that case I'll give you ten per cent of each pot for house charge and protection.'

'Indeed and I'll not be wanting a fancy man in the place.' Mike jerked his thumb to the other saloon across the street. 'Try Lew Martin. He's more your man I'm thinking. And now that's settled, will you be wanting a drink?'

'No thanks.' Dancer wasn't upset by the refusal. Mike Killigan had his own lay-out already nicely working. Lew Martin proved more amicable.

'I could use a good table man,' he admitted. 'Can you run a faro bank?'

'If I have to.' Dancer stared around the crowded saloon. 'But poker's my

44

game. Let me have a concession and we'll see how things turn out.'

Lew agreed and within an hour Dancer was sitting at a small baize-covered table ready to play with anyone who felt like chancing his luck. He would pay for his right to use the saloon by giving the owner ten per cent of each pot. That house charge would carry the privilege of food, a reasonable amount of drink and lodging in the upstairs rooms. It also offered the protection of the saloon bouncers who kept an eye on things in general and threw out awkward drunks.

Their help was appreciated but Dancer could have done without it. He had long ago learned how to defend himself and the small derringer he carried in a hide-away holster made him the equal of any gun-toting miner, cowpuncher or other Westerner he was likely to meet.

Life wasn't too bad at the Main Chance. Every morning Dancer went for a short ride on horse-back, returned to eat lunch and then settled himself down for play. Sometimes he would play until dawn, sometimes even longer, his face enigmatic as he dealt cards, raked in chips, lost or won as fortune and his skill dictated. Usually he depended on sheer skill, his knowledge of cards, men and probabilities. But he could bottom-deal if he had to and spent at least an hour each day manipulating the pasteboards.

The only fly in the ointment was the preacher.

His name was the Reverend Toole and Dancer suspected that the title was self-given. He roamed around the territory on a sway-backed mule — holding revival meetings, performing baptisms, weddings and funerals as the need arose. The gold pieces Rex had given him had tided him over and he had been religious in keeping his promise to see that the gambler had medical attention. Dancer had staked him to the mule and a warbag of provisions for no other reason than to get him out of the way and so get some peace.

'Your friend's hit town,' said Lucy Belle one morning. 'The preacher, I mean.' She smiled at the gambler, conscious of her attraction to men. She was a singer and at times helped out with the faro bank.

'Heaven save me from the zealous.' Dancer threw up his hands in mock despair. 'How long is he staying this time?'

'Why don't you ask him?' Lucy sidled closer. 'You know, Dancer, seems sort of like fate if you know what I mean.'

'No, I don't see what you mean.'

'Well, there's you and me and him.' She giggled. 'We ain't had a wedding in this town for too long now.'

'No!' Dancer liked the girl but that was all. He had no intention of letting things get out of hand. Quickly he changed the subject. 'Who was that big man arrived last night? The one with the sideburns and the plug hat.'

'Joe Lintaker?' Lucy looked serious. 'He's the big man in these parts. The

Indian Agent for the reservation.'

'The Apache reservation?'

'That's right.' She winked. 'He's making a good thing out of it too.'

'Is he?' Dancer slowly let a pile of chips fall from one hand into the other. 'Trading you mean?'

'Trading?' She gave a laugh. 'Well, I guess you can call it that.' She lowered her voice. 'I ain't sure, mind, and I'd hate to say so out real loud, but I think that Joe likes his job so much that he'd be willing to pay for it.'

'Like that, is it?' Dancer didn't press the question. Information could come slowly and he knew better than to display too much interest, Not that he was unduly interested anyway, the affairs of the Indians didn't concern him. Very little concerned him now aside from the pain in his lungs and the knowledge that his life was measured in smaller amounts than that of other men.

Trade was good that night and Dancer was busy. Deftly he dealt cards to three men, himself making the fourth. Two of them were cowpunchers who had ridden into town for supplies, the third a miner who had made a small strike, cashed in a sack of dust and was relaxing before going back to the hills. A bottle stood on the table and the air was thick with cigar smoke. Stakes were reasonable and it was a friendly game.

'Bid ten,' said one of the cowpunchers. 'You staying, Spur?'

'I'll stay.' Spur added his chips to the pile. The miner grunted, raised the bid ten dollars then grunted again as he sucked his cigar.

'Your twenty and ten more.' Dancer's slender fingers counted out a pile of chips and shoved them to the centre of the table. 'You staying, Roper?'

'Guess you're carrying too much weight for me.' Roper threw down his cards and helped himself to a drink. 'You lost many head lately, Spur?'

'I'm staying.' Spur attended to the financial details then shook his head. 'Not many. Are you?'

'I'll call,' said the miner. 'Show your hand.'

'Pair of aces.' Dancer threw down his cards.

'Two pairs.' The miner grinned triumphantly as he collected his winnings. The deal passed to Roper.

'Fifteen head gone last month,' said Roper. 'And we're only a small outfit They tell me that the Flying W lost over a hundred head during the past two weeks.'

'Rustled?'

'What else?' Roper paused in his deal to take a drink. 'Clive Leyburn's sworn to hang any rustler he catches with his own hands. He's going to brand anyone he catches with a running iron on his range, put it between the horns and drag him to the nearest town so they can hang him. I tell you things is getting bad.'

'Seems all your way,' said Spur thoughtfully. 'The Flying W, the Circle Bar, the Crossed Bit, all on the foothills.'

'That's why the boss asked me to check up while I was in town.' Roper seemed to have forgotten he was playing poker. 'If it's just a few head here and there there's nothing to worry about, steers are always getting themselves lost or maybe the tally was wrong, but when it comes to whole bunches then it's getting serious.'

'Sure is,' said Spur. The miner grunted.

'We playing poker or talking cows?' he demanded.

'Hold your hosses, old-timer,' said Roper easily. 'Don't let that little win go to your head. Before we're finished I'll be owning the socks off your feet.'

'Let's get on with the game,' said the miner. 'I ain't interested in beef.'

Neither was Dancer. He had little sympathy with anyone trying to steal cattle and less with anyone foolish enough to let himself be caught using a running iron to change a brand. The punishment Leyburn had promised, that of branding such a man between the eyes with his own iron before hanging him was drastic though just. The trouble was, as Dancer had discovered, that the cattle barons tended to regard the law as something they made for their own use and ignored when it went against them. Leyburn was quite likely to carry out his threat without opposition. The gambler shrugged and concentrated on the game.

The play was more or less even for a couple of hours with the gambler winning all the big pots and well ahead. The miner, after trying a weak bluff, threw in his cards and went over to the bar. The two cowpunchers, each with limited money and unlimited time, tried to stay in as long as they could before Dancer tired of the sport, took their last few chips by a skilful bluff, and then joined the miner.

Dancer turned as Lucy whispered in his ear.

'The boss wants you in the back room. Special game.'

'Who's playing?'

'The boss, Lintaker, the Indian Agent I told you about, and a Mexican from over the border.' She nudged him. 'Boss said to take things easy; don't lose but leave them their shirts.'

'I follow.'

Lintaker was a clumsy player, Lew Martin almost as good as was Dancer himself, and the Mexican, Lopez, so bad as to be impossible. And, yet, to Dancer's surprise, the man won slowly but steadily.

'Eet is good, theese game, no?' White teeth flashing, the Mexican raked in yet another small pot. '*Bravo, señores*, we play again, yes?'

'Sure.' Lintaker dealt the cards. 'How are things over the border, Lopez?'

'You are my ver' good friend, Señor Lintaker. To you I tell ze truth. Things, they are not so good. The Apaches,' he spat, 'they come against us and we can do nozings. The soldiers zey are asleep. Much trouble have theese Indians caused us. Many cattles, much beefs.'

He shook his head.

'Have a drink.' Lew pushed forward a bottle of whisky.

'*Gracias.*' Lopez drank the whisky as if it had been water. 'We play some more, yes?'

Later, when the game was over, Lew took Dancer to one side.

'Don't let what went on in there worry you,' he said.

'Worry me?'

'Well, doesn't it?'

'Why should it?' Dancer shrugged. 'If you want to let a Mex win a little money that's none of my business.'

'I guessed that you'd spotted it.' Lew hesitated. 'The fact is Lopez is an old friend of mine. Back in the old days he helped me a lot and now I'd like to help him. But you know these Mexicans and their pride. He's got an old mother, a sister, a wife and a dozen kids and yet if I was to offer him money he'd knife me. So I do the best I can. Once a month he comes here, I feed him, give him a drink and let him win a few chips at poker.' He spread his hands. 'It's the only way.'

'It does you credit,' said Dancer dryly. 'Is Lintaker in on the act too?'

'How do you mean?'

'Not much point in letting the Mex win if Lintaker takes it all off him again. That way you'd be paying off the wrong man.'

'I tipped Lintaker off,' said Lew after a moment. 'He knows as much as you do.'

'Sure.' Dancer didn't believe a word of what he had been told but he knew better than to argue. And it was none of his business what Lew Martin did.

'Everything all right then?' Lew seemed anxious.

'Why shouldn't it be?' Dancer shrugged. 'It's your money and you can do as you like with it. Me, I'm just satisfied to mind my own business, see nothing, say nothing and make no enemies.'

'That's the way to look at things.' Lew clapped the gambler on the shoulder. 'Tell the bartender to give you a bottle of the best stuff in the house. Tell him I said so.'

Dancer nodded and moved away. For a whim he ordered mineral water and when the bartender said he had none, settled for a bottle of the best brandy. He was carrying it to his room when a hand fell on his arm.

'Have you been seeing the doctor, my son?'

'Reverend!' Dancer sighed but could see that there was no escape. 'Come up to my room,' he suggested. 'You must be tired.'

'Tired and hungry,' admitted the preacher. 'Thirsty too.' He looked at the bottle.

'Strong waters Reverend?'

'Moderation in all things including moderation,' replied the preacher. 'A little alcohol can't hurt a man and it can do him a power of good. But moderation, always remember that. Moderation.'

'You won't let me forget.' Dancer led the way to his room. Shutting the door he produced two glasses, opened the bottle and filled each almost to the brim. Handing one to the preacher he lifted the other.

'To the new life,' he said.

'To a better world.' Reverend Toole touched the glass to his lips, looked pleasantly surprised and swallowed half the brandy at a gulp. 'Nice,' he said, wiping his mouth on a dingy handkerchief. 'It is a long time since I tasted such mellow spirit.'

'Drink up and have some more.' Dancer drained his own glass then, as pain seared his lungs, doubled up, coughing and fighting for breath. The glass fell from his hand as he fumbled for his handkerchief, covering his mouth as the spasms tore at his slender frame.

'Moderation,' said the preacher. His face was anxious.

'Don't give me a sermon.' Dancer wiped his lips, recovered his glass and tilted the bottle. 'So this stuff is bad for me, so what? What are a few more weeks or months or years to me?' He lifted the glass. 'A short life, Reverend, and a merry one. And if we all roast in Hell after it, well, isn't that better than living in Hell when you've got the chance to escape?'

'Sophistry.' Toole shrugged, 'I won't argue with you, Dancer, but down inside you I think that you know better than you say. Men are not wolves to rend and tear each other for the sake of physical comforts. There are higher things.'

'Forget it.' Dancer sat on the edge of the bed. 'What's the news?'

'Have you seen the doctor?'

'I said forget it.' A flush mounted on the gambler's thin cheeks.

'I was given a trust,' said the preacher with simple dignity. 'I must do my best to carry it out. Have you seen the doctor?'

'He called around again a week ago with some more stuff in a bottle.' Dancer gave a short laugh. 'He was wasting his time and I made him admit it. Medicine can't do me any good, not now, Nothing can do me any good. All I can do is to wait. Wait. Wait!' The glass suddenly splintered in his hand. Dancer stared down at the wreckage, the slivers of glass stained with blood welling from a slight cut at the base of his thumb. He dropped the splinters to a table, shook his hand and wrapped it in his handkerchief.

'Now what,' he said wonderingly, 'made me do a thing like that?'

'Don't you know?' The Reverend sipped at his brandy.

'If I knew would I ask?'

'A man can ask many questions if he doesn't want to admit that he knows the answers,' said the preacher. 'You know why you hurt yourself. It wasn't the fear of death, you've lived too long with that fear for it to have effect now. It was something deeper. It was the knowledge that you are wasting your life.'

'Should I buy a mule and follow your footsteps?'

'No. A man must believe in what he

preaches and you do not believe. But there are other ways a man can bring a little comfort to this world.'

'Charity?' Dancer shrugged. 'Name it, Reverend, and you can have it. How much?'

'Please!' Toole set down his glass, his face suddenly hard. 'Mock if you must but do not add insult to your mockery. I do not want your money.'

'Sorry.' Dancer shook his head. 'I didn't mean that. I guess that I've handled too much money and played against too many men who would have sold their souls for gold. Some of them don't own to possessing a soul anyway. It makes a man cynical.'

'I have seen some of these cynical men,' said the preacher. 'I've ridden far this last trip, as far as the Indian reservation. I do not like to think of what I have seen.'

'Indians?' Dancer shrugged.

'Indians are human, created in the same image as ourselves and worshipping the same God. They may call Him by a different name but Manitou, to them, is very close to our own faith. But even if they were utter savages they are men and women, not animals. They should not be treated as such.'

'Are they?' Dancer wiped his hand and examined the cut. It was shallow and would soon heal. 'I thought that they were happy on their own land. The reservation treaty gives them the right to govern themselves and forbids settlers entering their territory. What more do they want?'

'They want what was promised, not more and not less.' The preacher was serious. 'I have spoken to them, Dancer, and they are not easy in their hearts.'

'Who is?' The gambler changed the subject. 'Have another drink and tell me all the gossip. How many weddings, baptisms, funerals? Any new settlers moved in and how are your plans for a church getting along?'

'They aren't.' Toole looked a little shamefaced. 'I have done my best but

61

the business men are not interested. And I'm having opposition from other interests.'

'Because you aren't a fully qualified member of any organized church?'

'That is not true. I — '

'Skip it. What you are doesn't worry me.' Dancer reached for the bottle. 'Any news of Rex?' He stiffened at the other's expression. 'Well, is there?'

'Yes.' The preacher bent his head as if in prayer. 'I had forgotten. It is inexcusable, I know, but I am no longer as young as I was and at times my memory plays strange tricks. I had forgotten what I had to tell you.'

'Tell me? Rex sent a message?'

'No.'

'Have you seen him? Is he well?'

'I have not seen him. I passed through Twin Forks after leaving the reservation and picked up the gossip. Rex is in trouble, Dancer, bad trouble. He has powerful enemies who are working against him. I learned what I could but it was little enough.'

'And you didn't stop off to see Rex?'

'No.' The preacher stared directly at the other man. 'I am old and perhaps a little foolish but one thing I know. Sometimes a man's friends can help him best when his enemies do not recognize them. Had I ridden to see Rex the riders of the Flying W would have known that I was their enemy. As it is I am welcome in their bunkhouse. I feel that I can help Rex more by not seeing him.'

'By acting the spy, you mean.'

'As you wish. I am not ashamed of what I did. If to be a spy is to be loyal to a man who befriended me, then I admit to being a spy.'

'I meant no insult.' Dancer rose from the bed and paced the floor. 'Trouble, you said. Bad trouble?'

'Yes.'

'I was afraid of that.' The gambler halted and stared at the wall. 'It's been too long without word. We were pretty close in the old days and I'd thought — ' He shook his head. 'Never mind that now. The important thing is that Rex needs help.' He stared at the preacher. 'When can you ride?'

'At dawn.'

'So long?'

'My mule is tired and must have its rest. I am also tired though that is nothing. But the animal must rest.'

'At dawn then.' Dancer bared his teeth in a smile. 'Good enough. I can play through the night and pile up a stake.' He nodded as if coming to a decision. 'Go and get some rest. I'll meet you a mile down the trail at dawn. Move!'

Alone, the gambler took a long drink of brandy then, checking his derringer, went down to the saloon to his usual table.

Dawn found him, pockets heavy with gold, riding down the trail to Twin Forks.

4

Rex didn't like to remember how he had come home. During the war he'd toyed often with the concept, how he would ride over the rolling grassland up to the ranch-house, how maybe his father would come out to see who the visitor was, and Mark and Nancy and the boys of the Circle Bar would greet him and shake his hand and wish him welcome. There would be merry-making with a barbecue and perhaps tequila and dancing. There would have been a big homecoming with all the neighbours dropping in to chat and ask about the war and bring him up to date about the state of the range, the price of beef and the local news.

That was how it should have been. Instead he had staggered up to the ranch-house like a drunken man to collapse as someone opened the door.

Not that it was his fault. It had been dark when he'd recovered consciousness from Daren's blow. There was a thin wind and the coyotes were singing beneath a swollen moon. He'd lain for a long time, trying to ease the throbbing in his skull and dawn was washing the east with pink and gold when he'd finally managed to stagger to his feet.

Another hour had passed before he was able to move and then he'd discovered that his horse had gone, his saddle, guns and gear flung down beside the ashes of the long-cold fire. The boss of the Flying W had evidently taken what he claimed to be his property.

Had he taken the saddle and other gear Rex would have died. It took the water in the canteen and some whiskey from his bottle to restore warmth to his stomach and feeling to his bruised and battered body. He lit a small fire, forcing himself to swallow some sourdough cakes soaked in whiskey, then rolled up in his blankets as night darkened the skies again. The next morning he felt a little better but his head ached with a throbbing monotony and he knew that unless he could reach help he would die.

Unlike most Westerners Rex was used to walking. He'd learned the hard way, on forced marches and regular patrols. He could cover thirty miles a day if he had to with a bottle of water and a handful of parched corn, but that was when he was fit. Weak from his beating, suffering from concussion with over twenty miles to go before he could hit the Circle Bar ranch-house, he was in a bad way.

He left his saddle, saddle-bags and rifle. He left his spare clothing and personal gear. He took the canteen, the whiskey and his hand weapons and, as the sun climbed into the sky, he set out on his long trek.

He couldn't remember just what had happened during that journey. Heat and the effects of concussion had stolen his senses so that he wavered and fell and rose to his feet again without conscious knowledge of what he was doing. Once, he thought, he had shot a rattlesnake and eaten the reptile. Twice he had fired at lurking shapes waiting to pounce and eat the, as they thought, dying man. Again and again he had triggered the three quick shots which, in the West, was the common distress signal. And he forced his numb legs to carry him on and on and ever onwards across the deserted range.

It had been night when he'd finally hit the ranch-house. The building was in darkness and he'd half-staggered, half-run towards the door. He'd kicked at it, beaten at the thick panels with his gun butt then, as it yielded and light shone in his face, he'd collapsed.

That had been almost a month ago and he had only recently been able to stand on his feet.

'Feeling better, Rex?' Nancy, his brother's wife looking a little older and more harassed than he remembered, smiled at him as he walked into the kitchen. 'You want coffee?'

'Please.' Rex sat down. He had been walking around the out-houses and the effort had tired him. Soon, he knew, he would be fit again but common sense now dictated that he take things easy. 'You ready to talk now, Nancy?'

'Talk?' She paused in her task of pouring out the coffee. 'What about?'

'You know what about.' Rex leaned forward and took the cup. 'About the Flying W. About why the bunk-house is almost unlived in. About Mark.' He helped himself to sugar. 'Where is he, Nancy?'

'On a business trip.' She wiped her hands on her apron. 'He'll be back soon.'

'Are you saying that to calm me or for your own benefit?' He set down the cup and caught her wrist. 'When are you going to stop lying to me, Nancy? Don't you think I've a right to know the truth?'

'I've told you the truth.' She wrenched her hand from his grip. 'Mark went over the border to Mexico to arrange hiring some men. I told you that before.'

'Hiring Mexicans to work at the Circle Bar?' Rex shook his head. 'What kind of sense does that make?'

'Why ask me?' She didn't look at the big man. 'Ask your father, he's the one who knows what's going on around here. He's the one who found you. Ask him.'

'I will,' promised Rex. 'Where is he?'

'He rode down into Twin Forks a few days ago.' Nancy didn't raise her eyes from the floor. 'He should be back soon.'

'A business trip?' Rex waited for an answer. 'Listen, Nancy,' he said quietly, 'I'd like you to remember that I'm your brother-in-law. I'm one of the family and I've a right to know what goes on. When I left the Circle Bar things were a lot different to what they are now. We had men riding for us, Mark and you had just married and he'd never have left your side, Dad was where he should

70

be, on his range. Now look at things. Mark away, Dad away, only two riders left.' He shook his head. 'I don't get it.'

'You will.' Suddenly her voice was bitter. 'When you left, Rex, Clive Leyburn wasn't the boss of the Flying W.'

'I've met Leyburn.'

'Yes.' She looked at him and bit her lip. 'I know. You were delirious for a while,' she explained. 'You raved some and it wasn't hard to guess what had happened.'

'I know what happened,' he said grimly. 'Now I want to know why it happened.' He waited, staring at her, noticing how rough her hands had grown, how lank her hair, how dispirited her eyes. Six years ago she had been a lovely young girl, now she had somehow changed into a bitter woman. She must have guessed what was in his mind for she blushed.

'Things have changed, Rex,' she said. 'People have changed too.'

'Does the change have to be for the

worse?' Rex rose to his feet. 'Thanks for the coffee, Nancy. Maybe you'll learn one day that I'm to be trusted.'

She stared after him as he strode from the kitchen, memory tugging at her heart. Six years ago now she had had the choice of which brother she should marry. Rex had been quiet, solemn, intent on cattle, the range, the Circle Bar. Mark had been full of life, eager and willing for fun and with an attractive carelessness which had won her heart. Now? She sighed and began to clear away the things on the table. She was not the first woman nor would she be the last to learn that a husband should be a man, not a fun-loving boy.

The sound of a shot startled her and she ran to a window looking out towards the corral.

Rex stood there, tall and slender in his dark shirt, jeans, high boots and wide-brimmed hat. He had set a bottle on the corral fence and, as Nancy watched, his hand fell towards his belt, lifted the Colt from its holster, his thumb rolling back the hammer, releasing it as the barrel cleared leather.

Splinters flew an inch from the bottle.

'Good shooting,' she called. Rex turned and saw her.

'Is that what you call it?' He shook his head. 'I missed.'

'If that had been a man you would have hit him,' she said.

'Maybe.' Rex turned away and concentrated on what he was doing. He holstered his gun, let his hand fall free, tensed and went into the draw. His arm and hand operated in one smooth motion, his fingers curving around the butt as his thumb struck the hammer, the pistol lifting from the holster and levelling on the target as he pressed back the trigger, his thumb releasing the hammer at just the right time.

'Better,' called Nancy. The bottle had dissolved into a shower of splintered glass. 'Will you teach me to shoot, Rex?'

'What for?'

'Just for fun.' She went out to him

before he could object. 'I've often watched Mark practise but he doesn't shoot as you do. He holds the pistol and hits the hammer with his left hand.'

'You mean he fans the gun?' Rex crouched, his right finger pressing the trigger, the side of his left hand striking the hammer in a series of sharp blows. Each time he struck the hammer he cocked the pistol, the chamber revolved and, because of the held-back trigger, the hammer fired a cartridge. Rex had three shots left in the gun and he fired them so close together that the three explosions sounded as one.

'That's right,' said Nancy. 'He claims that he can fire faster that way.'

'Maybe he can.' Rex opened the side-gate of his pistol, ejected the used shells and reloaded with cartridges from his belt-loops. He loaded the gun with five shells, leaving one chamber empty. Colts had no safety catch and it was the custom to rest the hammer over an empty chamber to guard against accidents. 'I wouldn't say much for his accuracy though.'

'Does it matter?' Nancy looked at the fencepost. 'If you can shoot a man five times isn't that better than once?'

'Depends on where you hit him.' Rex crossed to the back of the kitchen and returned with five empty tin cans. He set them up in a row and took twenty paces from them. 'Not much use hitting a man five times, Nancy, unless you can down him. If you can do that then why waste the other four bullets?'

Rex raised the pistol and, rolling the hammer with his thumb shot down the five tin cans. Before the echoes of the shots had died away he was reloading the weapon.

'That was neat.' Nancy was a Westerner and as such had a normal interest in guns. 'You held back the trigger and used your thumb to cock the pistol. Mark was telling me about a fighter he'd met who'd had the triggers removed from his pistols. Would he use them the same way?'

'Yes.' Rex cocked the Colt and held it

poised in his hand. 'Where did Mark say he'd met this character?'

'Lamonte, I think. Somewhere like that. Why?'

'Removing the triggers is a gunman's trick.' Rex stooped, picked up one of the tin cans and tossed it into the air. As it began to fall he fired, cocked the gun, fired again and yet a third time. The tin, hit by each shot, jerked in the air and rolled on the ground.' He stared at the girl. 'Was Mark's friend a gunman?'

'He didn't say.'

'There seems to be a lot of people not saying very much around here.' Rex automatically reloaded his Colt. 'Even my father doesn't seem to want to see me.' He looked sharply at Nancy. 'Why?'

'How should I know?'

'Because you've spoken with him, that's why. Because you've lived here during the past few years and know what's wrong.' He slammed the pistol back into its holster. 'And don't tell me that there isn't anything wrong. I didn't get beaten up and almost killed just because I was a stranger. The name of Willard is hated in these parts. Why? Answer me, Nancy! Why?'

'Please.' She winced and Rex realized that he was gripping her arm. He relaxed and she stood watching him, rubbing her bruises. 'There is something wrong, Rex. I can't deny it. But I can't tell you what it is. Dan asked me not to tell you.'

'Why should my father do that?'

'I don't know. I think that he wanted to tell you himself.' She stared at something over the tall man's shoulder. On the trail a plume of dust rose as a traveller rode towards the ranch-house. Rex saw the direction of her gaze and turned.

'Two men and a buckboard,' he said. 'Would this be him?'

'It could be. He rode into Twin Forks with Jud and Curly.' Abruptly she gripped his arm. 'Rex. Promise me that you won't do anything rash.'

'What makes you think that I should

do anything like that?'

'Promise, Rex.'

'I promise nothing.' He shook off her arm and stood waiting for the buckboard to reach the house. As it came closer he could see that it was accompanied by a mounted man and a riderless animal was hitched to the tail-board. Curly Sorghum was riding while his brother Jud held the reins of the team, pulling the light wagon. They halted in a cloud of dust.

'Hi, Rex.' Curly slipped his saddle. 'Didn't know you were on your feet yet. How you feeling?'

'Better.' Rex glanced towards the buckboard. 'My father with you?'

'Dan? Sure.' Curly hesitated. 'Maybe you'd better go back into the house, Rex and let me and Jud handle him.'

'Handle him?' Rex stared at the cowpuncher. 'Is he hurt?'

'Well not exactly.' Curly seemed embarrassed. 'The fact is that the heat's got him down a mite. Jud had to take over and drive him back. But he'll be all right,' he said hastily as Rex stepped towards the buckboard. 'There ain't nothing wrong with him.'

'No?' Rex moved faster. Jud grinned when he approached, looking as uncomfortable as his brother.

'Hi, Rex, good to see you up and around again.'

'Thanks. What's wrong with my father?' Rex stepped forward as the cowpuncher rose and jumped from the buckboard. 'You heard what I said, Jud. Why didn't you answer?'

'Your dad's not himself, Rex,' said Jud quietly. 'I don't hold it against him and I figure that you shouldn't either.' He glanced into the buckboard, 'But he'll be all right.'

Rex didn't answer. He stared at the man sprawled out on the seat, eyes closed, mouth parted, his thin, lined face covered with sweat. Rex hadn't seen his father for six years. He had ridden away and left a big, hale, hearty man who had cut himself a living from the virgin prairie, fought Indians and rustlers, built up his herds against the elements, dug them out in winter and drove them to water in the burning heat of summer. Dan Willard had been a fighter, ready to tackle anything which walked or flew or crawled. But that had been six years ago. Something, had happened to the fighter since then. Somehow he'd given up the struggle and taken the coward's way out.

Dan Willard was drunk.

'How long?' Rex stared as Curly and Jud picked up the old man and carried him into the house. Nancy, standing at his side, bit her lips.

'I asked you a question.' Rex turned to face her. The others had gone into the house and he and the girl were alone. 'This isn't the first time, Nancy, is it? Jud and Curly told me that, not in what they said but how they said it. How long has my father been going into town and coming back hopelessly drunk? How long, Nancy?'

'Please, Rex.'

'Don't give me that, Nancy!' Anger

stirred within him so that his voice hardened and his eyes grew cold and bitter. 'I want the answer. You can give it to me or I can go out and find it myself. Damn it, girl!' He shook her so hard that her hair fell over her face. 'He is my father! Do you think I like seeing him like that?'

'Do you think that any of us like it?' her anger flared to match his own. 'Do I? Do Curly and Jud, the only ones who stay with us?'

'Does Mark?'

The question took her off balance. She stared at Rex, standing tall and hard and determined at her side and, for the first time since he had returned, admitted the ache inside her. Six years ago she had made a mistake. She had tried to forget it, to deny it, and had almost succeeded. Now, with her husband's brother standing beside her, she could deny it no longer.

'I don't know what Mark thinks,' she said dully.

'Do you care?'

'No.' She stared at him, her eyes wild. 'No, Rex, I don't care. Not now. Not now that you've come back and — '

'You are my brother's wife,' he said deliberately, and it was as if he had slapped her in the face. 'Six years ago you chose between us.'

'Is that what you are holding against me?' She stepped close to him, her arms reaching towards him. 'Six years, Rex! It's been a long, long time. Can't you forget and forgive?'

'Forgive?' He shook his head. 'There is nothing to forgive, Nancy. You had a choice to make, you made it. That was all there was to it.'

'And if I made a mistake?'

He didn't answer. He stood, head turned, listening to the sounds coming from the ranch-house. From one of the rooms a man was singing. It wasn't a good song and he wasn't singing it well but that wasn't his fault. Dan Willard was in no condition to do anything well. Dan Willard had been too drunk to even recognize his own son.

5

The room was of smooth planed boards, stained and polished with beeswax to a dull patina. Colourful blankets hung from pegs and curtains, now faded and frayed, hung over the windows ranked by their heavy shutters pierced with loopholes. On pegs hung weapons, an old percussion cap rifle, an older flintlock, one of the first Colt revolvers invented during the Mexican War way back in 1848. It was dull now, the once bright barrel rusted and dirty looking, the butt chipped and scarred as if by hard wear.

Dan Willard sighed as he looked at it, remembering when he had carried it at his waist, when he had used it during one of the Indian attacks when the Apaches had come riding against the house and the sultry afternoon had been filled with the smoke and fury of battle. Men had died that day. Red men and white both had died, their blood staining the rolling grasslands as the old culture clashed with the new. Fred had died that day an arrow in his throat and Luke, one of the hired men, dropped with his head opened by a tomahawk, his brains a grey-red mass. Or had it been Luke? It could have been Simon, or had Simon died later? Or earlier?

Dan sighed again, catching at fading wisps of memory, resentful because they were not as clear as they should be and events he had thought for ever impressed on his mind seemed vague and unreal as if they were fragments of a dream or snatches of a half-remembered tale told by some old-timer over his pipe. Dan had heard many such tales when a boy. Wonderful tales of the vast lands lying to the West, of beaver as thick as fleas on a dog, of bear and deer and antelope, of buffalo and the strange, savage tribes of Indians who trapped rare and costly furs and were eager to trade for iron pots, cheap guns, mirrors, beads, all the trinkets dear to the hearts of a primitive people.

Men had made fortunes in those days, going into the wilderness with a horse and a pack and a mule to carry that pack. Some had left their scalps to ornament the tepees of the tribes but others had come back loaded with furs and telling of the wonders to be found beyond the outposts of civilization.

Great days, wonderful days. All gone now. Gone with the memory of Luke and Simon and Fred and Angela. Poor Angela, the young girl who had been stolen by the Apache and had died in a manner no woman or girl or man either should die. Dan did not like to remember that and was glad that the details were vague. But one memory would never fade.

He fought it, denying it, not wanting the hurt it always gave. Martha, his wife, the mother of his sons, her face drawn and beaded with perspiration as she denied the agony which was tearing at her from an illness no one knew anything about. They had tried everything, hot cloths wrapped around her stomach, cold cloths, vile medicine from a travelling vendor of patent liquids which, so he claimed, would cure anything and everything up to and including the black fever. Nothing had done any good, not the doctor he had fetched over sixty miles of rough country, nor the prayers he had breathed while kneeling at her side. She had died and a part of him had died with her.

But his sons had lived on and on them he had based his hopes and ambitions. He had torn a ranch from the Indian country. He had imported cattle and watched them increase despite freezing winters and boiling summers. He had worked sixteen hours a day and his sons had worked with him. The Circle Bar was going to be the biggest, best, the strongest ranch in the entire country.

Then Nancy had come along and Mark had got married.

Then Rex had ridden away and the echoes of war had thundered over the West.

Then —

Dan groaned and tried to sit up. He fell back from the pain in his aching head and, after a while, tried again. A jug of water stood at the side of his bed and he gulped at it cursing the trembling of his hands which sent little droplets of water over the sheets. He set down the jug as a knock came at the door.

'Yes?'

'Coffee, Dan.' It was Nancy. 'You want some?'

'Please.' A good girl, Nancy. A fine girl. Too fine for that Mark. As fine a person as Curly and Jud and what he'd do without them Dan didn't know. The door clicked and he sat up, staring towards the open panel.

'Hello, father.' Rex stood and stared at the white faced old man in the bed. 'Recognize me?'

'Recognize you!' Dan frowned at his

son. 'Of course I do. You think I wouldn't know my own flesh and blood?'

'You didn't yesterday.' Rex stepped to one side as Nancy passed him with a tray bearing a pot of coffee, sugar, cream and two cups. 'Mind if I join you?'

'Glad to have you.' Dan licked at his lips. 'Yesterday?'

'You were carried home blind drunk.' Rex poured out the coffee, added cream and sugar to both cups, stirred and passed one over.

'Was I?' Rex hated the furtive expression in his father's eyes. 'Well, maybe I did have a little too much to drink, but hell, Rex, you know how it is. A man's entitled to have himself a bender once in a while.'

'Sure.' Rex sipped his coffee. It was too hot and he set it down. He took cigars from his pocket, lit one and offered his father one of the slim brown cylinders, 'Smoke?'

'No thanks.'

'Drink?' Rex took a flat bottle from his hip pocket. It contained whiskey and he opened it, smelt it and passed it over, 'Go on,' he urged. 'Take a hair of the dog which bit you. You won't be no good until you do.'

'Thanks.' Dan tilted the bottle and swallowed a good two inches of the raw spirit. Rex reached out, reclaimed the bottle and corked it.

'Now drink your coffee.'

Dan obeyed, his eyes watchful as he stared at his son. The whiskey had warmed him and settled his stomach. The hot coffee helped still more. Memories faded and the past retreated in the urgency of the present. Rex was home. Rex had already met trouble.

'Feel better?'

'Yes.' Dan could have done with another drink but didn't like to ask. That was cowardice, he knew, but it didn't worry him. He ran his tongue over his lips. 'You sure understand what's good for a man, Rex. Nancy, now, would never have slipped me a

89

drink. Women are funny about these things.'

'We've got to talk,' said Rex curtly. 'And I don't mean about the state of the weather. What's been happening while I've been away?'

'You fit yet, son?'

'Fit enough.'

'You was in a bad way when you arrived,' said Dan. 'Head all bloodied and bruised as if you'd been kicked by a horse. You was delirious too. Tell me, son, who was General Armitridge?'

'A hog that walked on its back legs.' Rex stared at the glowing tip of his cigar. 'He was in charge of the prison hospital and he hated the Confederacy.' He shrugged. 'Never mind that now. What about you?'

'The war must have been tough,' said Dan. 'Did you get wounded, son? You never wrote so as to let us know how you were.'

Rex sighed, looking at the man in the bed. Dan was almost sixty and a man aged fast in the West. Yet age alone wouldn't account for his furtiveness, his reluctance to speak out and his addiction to the bottle. He was, Rex knew, trying to avoid speaking of his own affairs and that was not like the man Rex remembered.

'The war is over,' he said. 'What happened then doesn't matter now. I'm home. I came home because I thought I could be of use and because I wanted somewhere to settle down and take things easy. I looked forward to it for two stinking years when I was rotting in the prison. When the war finished I didn't know whether to be sorry the South had lost or glad that I was to be released. I think I was just glad that the whole mess was over. So I came back. I bought a horse and some gear and rode home. I found a cold branding fire and was jumped on by Clive Leyburn and his boys of the Flying W. They said the horse was theirs, maybe they were right, but I had a bill of sale and was in the clear. Then they discovered who I was, they beat me up and warned me to

91

get out of the country.'

Rex looked at his hand. As he spoke his fingers had clenched until the cigar was a ruined mass of crushed tobacco. He threw it aside and lit another.

'As a home coming it wasn't what I'd anticipated.'

'I'm sorry, son,' said Dan.

'Sure you're sorry. So sorry that you go out and get drunk.' Rex rose from the edge of the bed and paced the room. 'So I'm almost a stranger, so all right. But I'm your son. Once that would have meant something to you. Once the Circle Bar and your family were respected. What happened, father? Did you lose your courage when I rode away?'

The taunt went home. Dan reared up in the bed, his thin features flushed with anger then, as Rex stared at him, he sighed and sank back again.

'I'd never have thought that a man could talk like that and get away with it,' said Rex. 'Not to you. The man who could call you coward and not have to pay for it hadn't been born when I left.' He stepped forward, his hands gripping his father's shoulders. 'Damn it, dad! What has happened around here since I left?'

'Plenty.' Dan licked his lips and Rex, sympathizing with the old man, held out the bottle. 'Thanks.' Dan returned it, accepted a cigar and sat, knees hunched, staring at the wall.

'You never met Clive Leyburn in the old days,' said Dan. 'He arrived about five years ago, just before the war started. He took the spread next to the Circle Bar and began to run cows on the range.' He made a little gesture. 'No harm in that. The range is free and there's plenty of room for all. Clive and me got on well enough and so did John, Clive's brother.' He drew at the cigar.

'John and Mark got on well. They were of an age and used to ride into town for a little fun. The two ranches operated most times as one. If there was any trouble at all it was caused by Daren, Clive's ramrod. He was too inclined to use his gun in an argument but Clive kept him in hand and there was no serious trouble.'

'So?'

'The war came and things got tight,' said Dan. 'We couldn't shift our beef and the herds began to increase out of hand. Water became short and grass as well. The Flying W and the Circle Bar managed to get along pretty well but we were both big outfits and both needed plenty of room. Still, Clive and me came to an agreement over the water and grazing, and we did manage to get one herd delivered to the railhead.'

'For the Confederacy?'

'Yes. We might as well have driven the beef away. They paid for it in paper money.'

'And now that money isn't worth the paper it's printed on.' Rex knew of the economic ruin which had followed the end of the war. The Confederacy had always been short of silver and gold and, without those precious metals to back its own currency, the paper was almost valueless. After the surrender it lost what value it had, and too many people found themselves loaded with worthless currency.

'That's right.' Dan sighed and shook his head. 'A heap of yellow-backs and you can't buy a bag of flour or a box of cartridges with it.'

'So you sold the herd, then what?' Rex was impatient.

'Things gradually got worse. We had cattle but we couldn't sell them. We couldn't hit the markets of the North and the South could only pay us in paper. The shopkeepers wouldn't take it or discounted it down to ten cents in the dollar. It was useless in Mexico. We had to have money to buy supplies, iron-work, saddles, stuff like that. We couldn't get cash money anyhow and the herds kept on getting bigger and bigger but at the same time, the stock was getting worse and worse.'

It was a familiar and inevitable picture the old man painted. The steers ran loose over the range, foraging for themselves on the buffalo grass which covered the prairie, drinking at the scarce water-holes and multiplying from the natural increase. This was normal. What wasn't normal was the amount of scrub bulls which were running among the herds, the amount of cattle which meant poor feeding and less water. The cows grew more numerous but they were poor animals with little meat and less stamina.

Normally their riders would cut out the unwanted bulls, weed out the prime steers for market and keep the herds down to a level where they could support themselves. But without any markets for their beef the cattle barons found themselves in the position of having vast herds but without money. Without cash they couldn't pay their riders and without riders they lost control of their cattle. It took many men to operate a drive, to work at round-up time, to do the branding and range-riding neccessary. Without riders the ranches became the easy prey of rustlers who could cut out a sizeable herd, run them over the border and sell them at give-away prices.

Such rustlers ran the double risk of the ranch owners and the Confederate troops who patrolled the Rio Grande on the watch for both smuggling and enemy agents. Beef was wanted by the Confederacy and, rather than let it go to the Mexican market, they would confiscate it. They would buy it too, but they couldn't offer anything but worth-less currency. The cattle barons were squeezed in an economic trap.

'I hoped that I could wait it out,' said Dan wearily. 'I knew that the war couldn't last for ever, and when it ended the North would be crying out for beef. I had a little money put by and as long as Clive and I could operate as a team it seemed that we could make out.'

'You didn't,' pointed out Rex. 'Why?' He had a sudden suspicion. 'Was it Mark?'

'Mark grew a little wild,' admitted

Dan. 'He took to playing poker down in Twin Forks and lost a mint of cash. I paid, what else could I do? I warned him, but he just laughed and said that he'd win it back.' Dan paused. 'I didn't realise just how deep he was getting. He gave IOUs to too many people, decent folk who I couldn't see go short.' He shook his head. 'I'll make it quick, Rex, your brother just about cleaned me out.'

'More fool you for letting him do it.'

'So you say and maybe you're right. But you reminded me a while ago that our name and the Circle Bar meant something to me. It did and it does. I couldn't see a son of mine unable to pay his debts. And I needed him, Rex. If I hadn't met his bills, he would have ridden away as you did.'

'And left his wife?'

'That wouldn't have bothered him none. From what I could see he and Nancy didn't get on any too well. Mark was restless and didn't see why he should stick around when there was excitement waiting to be picked up. He threatened to enlist more than once and with the riders leaving because of no wages I had to hold him as best I could.' Dan dragged at his cigar. 'If you'd have stuck by me, Rex, maybe things would have been different.'

'Maybe.' Rex paced the room again, admitting the truth of what the old man had said. He should have stayed. It had been wrong for him to have left because of a woman who had chosen his brother. But at the time it had seemed best. He halted and stared down at his father.

'Then what?'

'Mark came up with a plan. He suggested that he and John and Daren and a few of the boys should take a mixed herd over the border and sell them for what they could bring. We'd lose money, of course, but we would get paid in gold, and gold was what we needed. We could afford to take the loss so as to keep operating and we could build up the herds in pretty short time.

There was risk, of course, we had to run the patrols, but Mark reckoned he knew a trail and could make it.'

'Wait a minute.' Rex was remembering what Nancy had told him. 'Did Mark have any odd friends at that time?'

'He used to know a few Mexicans and drifters, nothing much.'

'You said that there was some rustling going on?'

'Some, sure. Why?'

'I was wondering how Mark knew of that trail he mentioned. Seems possible that he may have run a few head on a previous trip.'

'Are you saying that Mark was rustling?'

'No.'

'What makes you so sure?'

'Mark is my brother,' said Rex tightly. 'He could be wild, that I won't argue about, but he's no rustler.' He dismissed the notion. 'So Mark had a plan, did you agree with it?'

'There was nothing else I could do. I

was out of money and had to get some from somewhere. I talked to Clive and he took my word for it that Mark knew what he was doing. We cut out a decent sized herd and Mark, John, Daren and some of the boys headed over the border with them.' Dan wiped his face. 'We waited and waited. They got over the river and headed into Mexico, we learned that much from a rider who hurt his foot and had to return. He said that they'd had a little trouble but nothing serious.'

He fell silent and Rex, after waiting for a while, spurred him on.

'So they got into Mexico and I suppose they sold the beef. Then I suppose Mark came back with the gold.'

'No.'

'He didn't get the money?'

'He didn't come back,' said Dan bitterly. He looked at Rex. 'I'll tell it quick. Daren came riding back and he didn't come alone. He brought back the riders and he brought back John,

Clive's brother. He and the riders were on their horses but John was wrapped in a blanket.' He nodded at Rex's expression. 'That's right, he was dead, shot in the back.'

'And Mark?'

'Mark and the money had vanished.'

'I'm beginning to get the picture.' Rex drew fully at his cigar. 'What happened next?'

'We had a meeting. Daren told us that they had sold the beef and collected the money. They took almost three thousand head and got three dollars a head in gold. Nine thousand dollars, Rex.'

'Is that all?'

'It meant a lot to us. Half of it belonged to Clive and the Flying W, but never mind that. Daren said that Mark had got to drinking and wanted to stay a while south of the border. John didn't like that but agreed to stay for one night before returning. They got into a poker game — Mark, John and a couple of others. They played all night and when the game was over John had won everything Mark possessed, including the four thousand five hundred dollars belonging to the Circle Bar.' Dan took a deep breath. 'My money, Rex. Your brother threw it away over a card table.'

'Seems that Mark altered some since I left.'

'He had, Rex. He was the younger of you two, and he just went bad, I guess. Anyway, that is what happened. Mark had the gold in the safe at the hotel and he and John went to collect it. Daren and the others waited a while. Then Daren went out and came back with the news that John was lying dead in the street. They found him with a bullet in his back. The gold was gone. Mark was gone. Everything was gone.'

'Who told you all this?'

'Daren and the boys with him.' Dan shook his head. 'I know what you're thinking, Rex, but it wasn't like that. I rode over the border myself and I questioned everyone who could know of the affair. The hotel clerk said that

Mark had taken the gold from the safe and had given it to John, Later on he heard a shot. The livery stable told me that Mark had collected his horse and had ridden away that night. He had two saddle-bags and they looked heavy.' He sighed, 'I questioned Daren and his story held water. I asked the boys, and some of them were my own riders, their stories were the same. Mark lost at cards, handed over the gold and then killed John to get it back. That's what happened.'

'No,' said Rex. 'Not all.'

'No,' admitted Dan. 'There was Clive Leyburn. He thought a lot of his brother, Rex, and I can't blame him for what happened next. He swore that he'd get revenge one way or the other. He hunted Mark as if he were an animal but he could never catch up with him. He grew a little crazy I guess because he began to blame me for what had happened. It was my son who had robbed him, Rex, and there was only one thing I could do. I had to strip the range and sell everything I could to make it up. I paid Clive his share of the money Mark had stolen.'

'And then you had nothing left at all. You couldn't pay riders and so the range suffered. You've got cattle running without brands. You've got water and probably the Flying W is stealing it. You've still got the Circle Bar but you won't have it for long.' Rex stared at the Indian blankets on the wall. 'And Leyburn hates you, the Circle Bar and everything connected with you. He blames Mark for the death of his brother and probably blames him for all the rustling which is going on. And Mark? What of him?'

'We haven't seen him from that day to this. As far as I know Mark has just vanished.'

'Vanished? With all that gold?'

'We haven't seen or heard from him, Rex.'

'For how long now?'

'A year.' Dan shivered as if at the touch of a cold wind. 'A whole year, Rex.'

'And Nancy?'

'I told you, Rex. No one has seen or heard of your brother since the night when he killed John Leyburn and rode off with the gold.'

'A year.' Rex looked at his hands. 'Have you been hitting the bottle all that time?'

'I don't know.' Dan shivered again. 'It hit me hard, Rex, what Mark did. I was always proud of my sons and proud of my ranch. When you left me I leaned too heavily on Mark. When he went bad I had nothing left. The ranch had taken my life to build and I couldn't save it. The riders left me, Curly and Jud are staying on for board wages only and how long they'll stay I don't know. Every time I try to get back on my feet Clive or Daren steps in. So I took to taking a drink at the Golden Eagle and playing a little poker. Sometimes I win, sometimes I lose. Now and again I see Daren and every time I do he gives me a message from Clive. He warns me to find Mark or take his place. And I'm old, Rex, and I'm no good with a gun any more and I've got no one to back me up.'

'Yes, you have.' Rex drew a deep breath, filling his lungs and swelling his chest. 'You're not alone now, father. I've come back and I'm with you. Together we'll build up the Circle Bar.'

'You think so?' Hope flared in the old man's eyes to die as quickly as it was born. 'You can't fight the Flying W, Rex. They have everything. They have riders and money and men. And they have Daren.'

'Daren!' Rex clenched his hand, the knuckles showing white beneath the skin.

'He's poison, Rex. A natural born killer if ever I saw one.'

'He's a man,' said Rex evenly. 'And a man can die.'

'Maybe.' Dan sank back on his pillows. 'But a lot of men have died trying to prove it.'

Rex smiled briefly and left the room. Alone, the old man felt a sudden disgust with himself. He had felt self pity for too long, now it was time to alter his ways. He had fought before and could fight again and now he was not alone. Rex, his son, was with him.

He smiled and got out of bed, then tensed as gunshots echoed from outside. He crossed to the window, stared through it and frowned as he saw what Rex was doing.

The tall man was practising the draw, whipping his guns from their holsters and firing at a slender post set twenty yards away. Splinters flew as lead slammed into soft wood. But Rex, as Dan knew, wasn't really shooting at a post. He was shooting at an imaginary man.

Daren.

6

Clive Leyburn was standing at the corral when Daren came from the bunkhouse. The foreman was dressed in his best, his guns hanging low and tied to his thighs, his silk shirt matching his bandanna, a rattlesnake skin around his stetson and his high boots ornamented with bead-work. He carried a quirt in one hand and touched it to the brim of his hat as he saw the boss of the Flying W.

'Hi, Clive. Just going into town. Any messages?'

'No.'

'Not even the usual?' Daren glanced to where a group of cowpunchers stood against the fence post of the corral. Benson was among them. He met Daren's stare, his eyes without expression.

'No.' Clive scowled at the horses in the corral.

'You getting soft?' Daren's expression didn't alter but his voice held a sneer. 'Or maybe you figure that working Rex Willard over a little was good enough to pay for John's death.'

'Leave John out of this.'

'Why not?' Daren shrugged. 'He died with a bullet in the back, sure, let's forget him. Let's forget the living too, the man who shot him and stole your money.'

'I got paid.'

'Dan Willard paid you money. Did he give you a little extra to make you forget the death of your brother?'

'Watch it, Daren.' Clive stared at the foreman, his rugged face hard, his thick body set as for trouble. 'Don't let that tongue of yours run away with you.'

'Maybe you're the one to remember that.' Daren stepped closer. 'You're in a spot, Clive, and you know it. You've borrowed money on this spread and the only way you can hang on to the Flying W is to meet it when it's due. Can you do it?'

'That's my business.'

'Sure, so you can manage on your own. Maybe you can meet that note but if you do you'll wind up like old man Willard, drunk and broke and getting drunker all the time.' Daren smiled and called to one of the cowpunchers. 'Lem, saddle my horse, will you?'

'Sure, Daren.' The man jumped to obey. He went into the corral, caught the foreman's horse, saddled it, tightened the cinches and led it towards the ramrod. 'Here it is, Daren.'

The foreman nodded, not answering the cowpuncher. Lem hesitated, seemed about to say something then turned away. Daren looked after him then spat on the ground.

'No guts,' he said.

'Maybe he wants to keep his job,' said Clive.

'Eating dirt's no way to hang on to a job.' The foreman spat again. 'Better get rid of him and Benson too.'

'I do all the firing and hiring around here,' reminded Clive. 'Don't push me too far, Daren. I may remember that I'm the boss and I'm the one to say what goes.'

'You made me ramrod for a reason,' said Daren coldly. 'You and me both know that reason. You're big, Clive, and you look tough but we both know that deep down inside you're weak. John used to back you and you got by. Now I back you. Without me you'd make it up with old man Willard. Without me you'd grow soft and forget that the only way a man can get on in this country is to be hard and strong. You can't be friends with the other cattle owners, Clive, not unless you want to be squeezed out. You've got to hold what you've got and hold it with the power of your guns if need be. Soft talk'll get you nowhere.'

'Keep your voice down, damn you!'

'I know what I'm doing.' Daren didn't alter the tone of his voice. 'If you want to call me, Clive, you can do it at any time. But until you do you'll eat dirt if I say so because you know that

I'm the better man.'

'Quicker on the draw, Daren, that's all.'

'The one that walks away is the better man,' said the foreman easily. 'But quit worrying, Clive. I'm with you, always have been and maybe I always will be. With me behind you, you can smash Willard and the other small outfits. Then you can smash the big outfits and own all this part of the country.'

'You're too generous,' sneered Clive. 'Where do you come in?'

'I'll arrange my own side of the affair. You could make me a partner, Clive, it's been done before. Or you could make me your heir.' The foreman grinned. 'Now that John is dead you've no kin and no one to leave the spread to if you die.'

'I'm not quite a fool, Daren.' Clive smiled and leaned against the fence. 'If I made you a partner or my heir I'd be begging for trouble. How long do you think I'd live, Daren, if you had an active interest in my demise?'

'How long do you think you'll live if I've no reason for your existence?' Daren smiled, not at all put out by the other's remarks. 'Let's not get hot under the collar about this thing, Clive. This is a big country and there's plenty for all.'

'So you keep telling me.'

'Then think about it.' The ramrod smiled again, swung into his saddle and controlled his restless mount. 'I may be a couple of days. There's a new gambling man I aim to lock horns with. If I see Willard I'll tell him to keep his spawn off the Flying W. If I find him on our territory I'll fix him for good.'

Clive sighed as he stared after the foreman. Daren was both valuable and a nuisance. He was hard and was growing harder. He was also growing impatient. As a foreman he knew his work and did it well and as a gunman he knew no equal. The Flying W owed as much to Daren as to the official owner and, in the beginning, Daren, John and Clive had been friends. It had been a mistake, Clive could see that now, but it was too late to do anything about it. Daren knew too much.

He knew, for example, about the loan. Things had been desperate when Mark had announced his plan and Clive had been eager to join in. Then, when John had been murdered and the money gone, he had been forced to find fresh capital. Money was tight in the southern states and the few willing to lend could state their own terms. Clive had been approached by a man and offered a round ten thousand dollars on terms which would make him a virtual employee of the lender. He had accepted. Daren had advised him to take the money and accept the terms. Now, unless he could meet the payments, he would lose all that he had worked for.

But, as Daren had said, it was worth the gamble. He could retain his riders, increase his herds and widen his spread. He had already swallowed up a few of the smaller outfits, pressing them until they had to sell or run. Daren had arranged that, riding at night sometimes and returning with a lathered horse and tainted with the smell of burning. Clive had wanted to protest but, as the foreman had pointed out, basically he was weak. He was afraid of losing everything and so sat back and let the foreman take more and more control of the ranch.

But weak or not Clive was no fool. It suited him to let Daren think that he was working for himself. The man was a paid employee, a hired hand, no more, and as such could be fired at any time. Let him work and build up the Flying W. Let him kill and burn and terrify the small ranchers. When he had built the Flying W up into a cattle empire then Clive would strike. The foreman would be paid off, sent packing and things would settle down to a peaceful routine.

That had been his plan. The death of John had upset it for a while but nothing had really altered. Let Daren imagine that he was the real boss and then, when things had changed for the better and cattle was worth high prices again, Clive would act. He would sell out to a syndicate in the east and retire to live a life of ease on his wealth.

The vision cheered him as it always did. He smiled, then frowned as he remembered his murdered brother. He needed John now more than ever. John had been the only man he felt he could trust, the only one who sympathized with him. He would understand why he was using Daren. John would have known how necessary it was to build high and big no matter what the cost so that they could be secure in the future. But John was dead and Clive's hatred of the Circle Bar smouldered into fresh life as he thought about it.

Angrily he went into the house.

Benson, leaning against the corral, stared after him then at Lem.

'Sure didn't take you for a foreman's carpet, Lem,' he drawled. 'You near bust a gut saddling that horse.'

'Daren ordered me to do it,' said Lem uneasily.

'Since when has a ramrod been entitled to a valet?' One of the other cowpunchers took a toothpick from his mouth and spat in the dust.

'Leave me alone.' Lem dragged his boot in the dust. 'You know Daren, when he wants a thing, he wants it.'

'You sure help give it to him.'

'Quit riding him,' said Benson suddenly. 'If he wants to live his life that way then it's his funeral. So let him eat dirt for the ramrod. What's it to us?'

'That Daren!' One of the men shrugged. 'He'll meet a rannie one day who'll call his tune. Man, what a day that'll be.'

Unconsciously they all turned and stared down the trail at the dwindling figure of the foreman.

Daren neither noticed their stares or if he had they wouldn't have bothered him. He had a tremendous contempt for most of the human race, a contempt which he found hard at times to

118

control. Power had fed that contempt, the power of the guns he carried low on his thighs. He had learned the power a Colt could give early in life. He had faced a local bully, outdrawn him and watched as the man had kicked out his life in the dust of a small town street. That had been only the beginning.

Daren was naturally fast and had practised hard to make himself faster. He could draw and shoot and put his bullets where he wanted them to go. Like most successful gunmen he had learned that accuracy was more important than sheer speed, that the man who could make his first shot count was more to be feared than one who could draw a shade faster but who needed a burst of firing to hit his opponent.

But being able to draw and shoot was not enough. A gunman had to want to kill. He had to want to face danger and pit his skill and speed against those of others. There was a fascination about it, a thrill, an experience which could get hold of a man like a drug so that he wanted to kill and kill and kill for the sheer animal lust of destruction.

Daren had reached that stage long ago.

Now he rode towards Twin Forks, slouched easily in the saddle, his eyes and mind alert as they were always alert for any possible signs of danger. As he rode he reached into a pocket, took out tobacco and papers, rolled a cigarette and stuck the quirley into the corner of his mouth. He flared a match against his thumbnail, lit the cigarette, killed the match and breathed smoke.

He was thinking of Clive.

Daren had nothing but contempt for the owner of the Flying W. The man was a coward, nothing more, a man afraid to reach out and grab for what he wanted. Daren had done the dirty work so far and he was aware of Clive's opinion of what he had done. He was also aware of the position Clive thought he occupied. His smile grew thin and cruel. If the boss of the Flying W ever tried to kick him off the ranch then he was due for an unpleasant surprise. Daren might go, but if he did it would be feet first and he had confidence enough in himself to know that that wouldn't happen.

He stiffened as a figure cut towards the trail then relaxed as he recognized the old man on the sway-backed mule.

'Good afternoon, sir.' The Reverend Toole doffed his hat as the foreman joined him. 'My eyes are not as good as they were but I thought I recognized you.'

Daren nodded. 'Going up to the ranch?'

'I was thinking of calling, sir. That is if you have no objections?'

'Suits me,' said Daren easily. Hospitality was a part of Western culture and any rider could call at any homestead and ranch-house for a meal. In return he was asked only that he caused no trouble and also did not outstay his welcome. The preacher, Daren knew, depended on such charity to keep going. 'Haven't seen you around lately,' he said. 'Where have you been?'

'Spreading the Word,' said the preacher. 'I've been into the mountains as far as the agency and have swung around almost to the Rio Grande.'

'Into the reservation, eh?' Daren stared at the old man through a veil of cigarette smoke. 'What took you there?'

'My work.' Toole had a simple dignity which nothing could shake. 'I've tried to bring comfort and peace of mind to the Indians. They are suffering, sir, as few men should suffer.'

'They're Indians,' said the foreman contemptuously.

'They are human,' corrected Toole. 'They are sick and hungry and dread the winter when many must die. It is not good to see these things.'

'Then look the other way.' Daren was cynical. 'You've enough to do riding the range and calling at the ranches without worrying your head about a bunch of Indians.' Daren flipped away his cigarette. 'You called at the Circle Bar yet?'

'Not yet.'

'Intend to?'

'If my path lies that way then I shall call. I hope to call everywhere I could be needed but this land is so big and the people so scattered that it will take time.'

'I'd like you to make time,' said Daren. He smiled, a thin, cold, humourless smile. 'I'd like it very much. Why don't you go straight there now instead of to the Flying W?'

'For what reason, sir?'

'I want you to take a message.' Daren breathed deeply, his nostrils flaring. 'Tell Willard that any time his cub wants to see me then I'm willing. Tell him that and tell him from me.'

'I do not wish to carry a threat, sir.'

'No?' Daren stared at the old man. 'Maybe you'll remember that when you ask at the bunkhouse for a bed and a plate of chow. I can be generous, preacher, and I can be the other thing. A man who refuses to do a simple errand for me ain't exactly a man I'd call my friend.'

'I am not to be bought with food and a bed, sir.' Toole stared the foreman straight in the eyes. 'Nor am I a man to be used for evil purposes. If you have an errand then I shall be happy to accommodate you, but I will not carry a threat of murder.'

'Murder?'

'You are well known in these parts, sir. May I remind you that a man of strength should also be a man of charity. To kill is easy, to withhold death is sometimes hard.' Toole frowned at the ears of his mule. 'This Willard, he has offended you?'

'You could say that.' Daren bared his teeth in a snarl. 'Listen, you old fool, and listen good. I want you to ride to the Circle Bar and deliver a message for me and I want no arguments about it. Tell Willard that if his cub thinks that he has a grievance against me then I'm willing to let him settle it.' He gave a short laugh. 'That ain't a murder threat, preacher. I'm willing to stand up against him man to man. If he wants to come shooting then that's up to him. If he wants to forget it then I won't argue.' He laughed again. 'But if he wants to eat dirt then that's up to him. If I see him in town then that's just what he'll have to do.'

'I see.' Toole eased himself in his saddle. Things were working out better than he had hoped. As yet he had not dared to contact the Circle Bar for fear that word would be carried back to the Flying W. Now Daren was ordering him to do exactly what he wanted. His token resistance had only made the foreman more determined that the old man should obey.

'When you've done it,' said Daren carelessly, 'you can bring back his answer. Wait at the Flying W until I get back if I ain't there when you arrive. Tell the cook to see that you get everything you want.' His eyes became shrewd. 'And listen, preacher, if you have anything of interest to tell me then maybe there'll be a little gold in it for you. Understand?'

'I think so,' Toole controlled his anger. 'You want me to act the spy for you, is that it?'

'Right between the horns,' said Daren easily. He touched spurs to his mount. 'Be seeing you.'

Toole stared after the foreman as he rode away then thoughtfully dug his heels into the mule and turned the patient beast from the trail leading to the Flying W. Before him the soaring majesty of the Apache Mountains reared towards the sky, now the limited home of the Indians who had once roamed all over the south-west, raiding the Mexicans, the settlers, the ranchers and homesteaders who had come pouring into their lands. Now they had retreated, living in uneasy peace in the lands granted to them by the white man's treaty.

The Circle Bar lay to the West of the Flying W, the two ranches several miles apart. Toole jogged on his new path, his mind turning over what he had seen and learned on his travels. After he had taken the news to Dancer he and the gambler had come to Twin Forks. The gambler had stationed himself at the Golden Eagle where he was building himself a reputation as a cool poker player and one who ran a square game. Toole himself had drifted over to the Indian agency and into the reservation where he had talked to the Indians.

They were, as he had told Daren, restless. The agent, Lintaker, was not a good man for the job. He was careless, indifferent to the wants of his charges and thought more of filling his own pockets than taking care of the Indians. It was his job to provide beef and blankets, flour and other supplies to the tribes in return for their agreeing to remain in the reservation. Deprived of their normal hunting and raiding way of life the Apaches could no longer hunt buffalo, steal cattle and war with other tribes as they had done for centuries. The treaty they had signed with the white man guaranteed that the agent would provide the supplies.

But as yet he had not done so. Some cattle had been given to the Indians but not enough. As yet they had managed to eke out their diet with game and wild berries gathered during the summer. But with the approach of winter they were growing worried at the lack of beef to smoke and store for the cold months. Toole had tried to explain that the agent would continue to supply beef through the winter but the Indians hadn't believed him. They had hinted darkly of war and raiding and broken treaties and when Toole had spoken of it to Lintaker he had laughed, slapped the gun at his thigh and informed the old man that he could take care of himself and as many damn savages as thought different.

Toole sighed, jolting back to awareness as his mule stumbled on the trail.

Before him, low on the horizon, the buildings of the Circle Bar offered a warm welcome.

7

Nancy was busy making soap when the preacher arrived. She had collected all the fat used in the house and had let it soak together with wood-ash in a huge wooden tub. Now she was washing out the lye, settling the converted tallow which she would later wash with vinegar to nullify the caustic. She smiled at the old man as he slipped from his mule, greeting him as she would any stranger.

'Hi, there. Step down and rest awhile.'

'Thank you kindly, madam.' The preacher stared at her, liking what he saw. 'Is Rex around?'

'Rex? You know him?'

'We've met, madam. Is he available?'

'He's over at the corral.' Nancy glanced up at the sun. 'You'll stay for something to eat?'

'Thank you.' Toole smiled at her, led his mule to a patch of shade, and hitched it to a rack.

'Unsaddle and turn it into the pasture,' called Nancy. 'May as well let it eat while it's waiting.'

The preacher nodded his thanks and did as she suggested. The mule snorted as he turned it into the pasture, stretching its neck as it cropped the lush grass reserved for the milk cows and harness animals.

Rex was over at the corral with his father and the two cowboys. He smiled as Toole approached and held out his hand.

'Preacher! Good to see you again.' He introduced Toole to the others.

'You're welcome,' said Dan. He had changed since his talk with Rex. Now he stood straight and tall again, his skin had regained its healthy tan and his eyes were bright. He looked what he was, a man who had regained hope and a mission in life. 'Any friend of Rex is welcome at the Circle Bar.'

'Perhaps you would wait until I've delivered the message that I carry before saying that.' Toole repeated what Daren had told him to say. 'I'm sorry, Rex, but it was a good excuse to ride over and see you.' He glanced at Curly and Jud. 'If we could talk alone?'

'I can trust everyone you see,' said Rex. 'But we'll talk later. Just now we're busy with the horses.' He turned back to the corral. Inside the fenced enclosure a score of semi-wild horses snorted and pranced as the two brothers roped and haltered them. Breaking them in would take time but the effort would be worth it. Rex had collected them from the range, the offspring of a bunch which had broken free from the corral and run away a couple of years earlier.

'Leave it now, boys,' he called. 'Let them settle down a mite and get used to a rope around their noses. We'll start breaking them in tomorrow.'

'Weren't you going to tally the herd tomorrow?' Curly, his hat pushed back on his forehead, smiled with a flash of white teeth. 'You've got a job there big enough to keep even you happy.'

'That can wait.' Rex led the way towards the cookshack where Nancy was standing beside an iron tripod. She beat the iron and called out the regulation summons to eat.

'Come and get it!'

Over the meal Toole learned what had been happening at the Circle Bar.

'We've worked like slaves to get the ranch in some sort of order,' said Rex. 'That's why I've not been able to ride over to Lamonte and see Dancer. I couldn't do much the first few weeks and have been trying to make up for lost time.'

'And he's made up for it too.' Jud helped himself to more beans and pork. 'Up at dawn, cutting out the scrub bulls, branding the mavericks, tallying the herds, collecting the horses, man, you should see him go!'

'You've done your share,' said Rex. 'Everyone's done their share.' He leaned back and looked at the preacher. 'Surprised that you haven't been this way before.'

'I can explain that.' Toole sipped at his coffee. 'I was calling when I heard what had happened to you.' He shook his head at Rex's instinctive denial. 'I heard it at the Flying W. A man named Benson was saying that it was a low-down thing to have done. He didn't get much support. Afterwards I spoke with him and he told me what Daren and Clive Leyburn had done. He was thinking of leaving the Flying W and joining you but I talked him out of it.'

'Why?'

'I thought that he would be of more help to you where he was.' Toole made a gesture. 'Not as a spy, he wouldn't do that but there was talk of riding down here and burning you out. I thought that a man who could send word if that was to happen would be valuable.'

'Well?'

'I thought that same about myself. I heard in town that you had reached home and that you were well but in trouble. So I told Dancer and we both came down here.'

'Dancer came with you?' Rex craned his head. 'Where is he?'

'In Twin Forks. He told me not to ride up to you unless I had a good reason. He's busy collecting information down at the Golden Eagle.'

'Wait a minute!' Dan leaned forward. 'I don't get this. In my book a man's friends are to be found at his side.'

'Dancer was an intelligence officer during the war,' said Rex. 'Intrigue is in his blood. He knows what he is doing.'

'Seems to me that he'd be more useful right here on the ranch,' said Curly. 'I've met him, a smooth, fancy man with a way at cards. Didn't take him for a friend of yours, Rex, not by the way he talks.'

'That's right,' said Jud. 'He seems to be a friend of Daren's and the Flying W more than the Circle Bar.'

'I can explain that,' said Toole. 'I thought that we should have come directly to you but Dancer said that that would be wrong. He said that we should bide our time. He told me to tell you, Rex, that this is more than just a matter of you getting revenge on Daren, he's found out something and wants to find out more. When he does he'll come out in the open.'

'I can trust Dancer,' said Rex.

'What are you going to do about Daren?' Dan looked worried. 'He's a fast man with a gun, Rex. Damn fast.'

'Maybe I can slow him down.'

'No.' The preacher was definite. 'Don't do it, Rex. Daren wants you dead for some reason. I could tell that. If you meet him in town and you are armed he will kill you. If he meets you without a gun then he will deride you. Either way he will gain his own ends. Once you eat dirt then you'll have no respect in this part of the world.'

'I won't eat dirt,' said Rex. He clenched his hands. 'And I'm not afraid of Daren either. I'll meet him any time, the sooner the better.'

'No!' Nancy pressed her hand to her lips, her eyes huge against the pallor of her face. 'No, Rex! He'll kill you!'

'I've got to meet him,' said Rex. 'If not now then later. I've got to accept his challenge or ride out of the country. You know that, dad.'

Dan nodded, his face heavy and haggard with dread. He did know it, it was a part of the West. With no courts and few law-makers men carried their own law at their belts. Gunfights were the accepted way of setling feuds and no man could retain his respect if he refused to meet a challenge.

But Daren was fast. Dan was afraid that he was about to lose his remaining son.

'Violence never does good,' said the preacher. 'Daren is a killer, I saw it in his eyes. Why give him what he wants?'

'Am I?'

'If you go against him you are.' Toole looked at the others then stared at Rex. 'Sometimes it pays to look a little deeper than the obvious. That is what

Dancer did and why he is not now at your side. That is what I, in my small way, have done and why I rode to tell Dancer the news instead of coming here to nurse you. Why should Daren want to kill you?'

'I showed him up in front of his boss,' said Rex. Briefly he told what had happened when he'd ridden back home. 'I pulled a gun on Daren and made him back down. A man like him could never forgive a thing like that.'

'Admitted, but why didn't he force you to draw when he had the chance?'

'Clive warned him that there was to be no shooting.'

'Clive Leyburn is not what I would call a strong man,' said the preacher. 'Daren is. I do not think that the loss of his job would stop him from doing what he wanted to do.' He paused, frowning in thought. 'Yet he struck you, left you to make your own way home or die. It would not have been a clean death but it would have left him unresponsible for your end. You managed to live and you reached home.'

'He wasn't to know that I could do that.'

'No, but either way his ends were served.' Toole looked apologetic. 'Pardon me for saying this but it is common knowledge that your father had let grief and worry weaken him.'

'I was fast becoming a drunk,' said Dan. He stared at the preacher. 'Don't mind your words, Reverend. I deserve them.'

'Perhaps.' Toole made a slight gesture. 'I am not concerned with the reasons, only the outcome. You were weak and not dangerous. Rex came home and he was a danger. So he was beaten up and left either to live or die. Had he died the second blow would have finished what the actions of your younger son had started. Even his arrival, half-dead, injured, raving perhaps with delirium, served its purpose. It was a warning not to tamper with the Flying W. You ignored that warning and,

138

from what I can see and have heard, you are busy putting the Circle Bar back on its feet again. So Daren sends you a challenge and if you answer it he hopes to kill you.' Toole looked hard at the tall man. 'Doesn't it seem as if there is a little more behind this than meets the eye?'

'I'm beginning to see what the preacher is getting at,' said Curly suddenly. 'Tell me, Boss, have you got a note on the ranch?'

'A mortgage? No.' Dan shrugged. 'No one would give me one if I wanted it.'

'So they can't be trying to get your spread by ruining you so that you can't meet the payments.' The cowpuncher looked deflated, 'Then I don't get it.'

'I think that you could be on the right track,' said Toole. 'If they beat the Circle Bar down into the dust what is to stop them moving in and taking over? With Mark missing, Rex dead and Mr Willard a drunkard, beaten by fate and sorrow, Leyburn could run his cattle on Circle Bar range, feed them on Circle Bar grass and take over the water holes.' He looked at the rancher. 'Tell me, Mr Willard. If the Flying W did move in like that what could you do?'

'Fight.'

'But you have only two men, three with Rex, not counting yourself. How hard could you fight?'

'I'd get Leyburn,' snapped the old man. 'I'd do that if it was the last thing I did.'

'Now, yes. But a little while ago?'

'I see what you mean,' said Dan slowly. 'No one fears a drunk.'

'If Rex had died or if you had been scared of the warning then the Flying W could have simply moved in without gunplay. In fact they could have made it quite legal by buying you out for a nominal sum.' The old preacher nodded as if he had arrived at the logical and only explanation of what had happened. 'Several smaller ranches have been swallowed by the Flying W as it is. The

Circle Bar is a big spread even though you have few men to run it. But it is still yours. If Leyburn could make it his then he would own all the range this side of the Apache Mountains.'

'With the war over there's going to be a big demand for beef.' said Jud abruptly. He grinned. 'That's why me and Curly have stayed on without pay. We figure that when the wheel turns and we hit the jackpot we'll collect but good.'

'You're lying,' said Dan without rancour. 'You're only staying because neither of you has the fool sense to get out and earn some good wages.'

'That's right,' said Curly. 'We've got a soft boss and we know it.'

Both cowpunchers laughed and Dan and the others joined in. Curly and his brother had remained because of sheer loyalty to the old man but both would have died rather than admit it. Rex became serious.

'You make sense, Reverend. Is that what Dancer thinks?'

'Yes, some of it anyway.'

'I can't believe that of Leyburn,' said Dan slowly. 'We used to be friends. I can understand him feeling bitter over the murder of his brother but to turn on me like that and want to smash the Circle Bar — ' He shook his head.

'Men are peculiar,' said Toole. 'They can go on for years being nice, decent people and then, quite suddenly, they can change. From being satisfied with a little they can begin to want a lot. They get power-mad, gold-hungry and nothing is allowed to stand in their way. The tragedy is that, once they have got what they want, they realize that the price they paid was far too high.'

'Yes,' said Rex. 'I suppose they can.'

'Where are you going?' Nancy rose to her feet, her eyes anxious.

'Where do you think?' Rex slowly slipped each of his Colts from their holster, checking on the weapons and spinning the chambers. He slipped them back, drew them with a speed which made Curly gasp, then settled them on his thighs. 'The preacher brought me an invitation,' he said. 'Remember?'

'You can't go, Rex!' Immediately the girl was at his side. her fingers digging into his arm. 'You mustn't go! I won't let you!'

'Please, Nancy.' He released her fingers.

'You'll be killed!' She looked at Dan trying for his support. 'Stop him!'

Dan didn't answer.

'He can't stop me,' said Rex evenly. 'And he wouldn't if he could.'

'Then you stop him!' She stared at Curly, at Jud, then at the preacher. 'You can't see a man go to his death.'

They remained silent.

'Listen Nancy.' Rex put his finger beneath her chin and tilted her head so that she was forced to look at him. 'There are some things a man simply has to do. Daren has made the call and I've got to face it. He's probably down in Twin Forks now boasting that he has me and the Circle Bar on the run. If he gets away with it then we'll be cold meat for anyone and everyone who fancies his weight. I've got to call him, Nancy, for that if for no other reason.' His face hardened. 'But there is another reason.'

'He's right, Nancy,' said Dan. 'He's got to do it.'

'You!' She stared at them, then, suddenly, her face crinkled and she ran into the house. Rex stared after her, hard-eyed, then turned to his father.

'I may come back,' he said evenly. 'Or I may not. Either way we carry on as we started. The Circle Bar stays what you made it.'

'Want us to come with you?' Curly glanced at his brother.

'No.' Rex grinned. 'There's too much work to do without you two finding an excuse to slope off into town. Once you taste the fleshpots there's no telling when you'll be back.'

'Killjoy.' Curly grinned, then became serious. 'Watch for his left hand, Rex.'

'I'll remember it.' Rex nodded, stared

around for a last long look at the familiar buildings, then went to collect his horse. Toole joined him as he started down the trail.

'Mind if I ride with you?'

'Why not?' Rex grinned. 'A preacher could be handy at that.'

'Death is too serious a matter to joke about,' said the preacher severely. 'And a man riding out to kill or be killed should find more to think about than jokes.'

'Don't fool yourself, Toole.' Rex became serious. 'I know what I'm facing. But would it surprise you to learn that I have every confidence in the fact that I will be the one to walk away?'

'Daren is fast.'

'Sure, so everyone keeps telling me. But is Daren a good shot?'

'I don't follow.'

'You will.' Rex glanced up at the sun then spurred his mount to greater speed. 'Jerk up that mule, Reverend. We want to get in before dark.'

'I'm hurrying as fast as I can.' The

preacher wiped his steaming forehead. For a while they rode in silence then Rex halted, staring towards the looming bulk of the mountains.

'What is it?' The preacher, glad of the chance to rest, reined in his mule. 'What can you see?'

'Buzzards.' Rex pointed towards the horizon. 'See?'

'My eyes aren't good,' apologized the old man. 'But what of it? Buzzards always circle in the sky.'

'Not always,' corrected Rex. 'Only when they see something almost ready for the eating.' He struck spurs into his horse, turning its head towards the small black dots. 'Come on.'

The horse was faster than the mule and Rex had dismounted by the time the preacher joined him. The tall man was stooping over something lying on the ground. He looked up as Toole slid from his mule.

'Get water and that bottle of whiskey I carry in my saddle-bag. Hurry!'

'What is it?' The preacher hurried to

obey. He carried the canteen and bottle towards the tall man. 'What is wrong?' He caught his breath as he saw what was lying on the ground.

It was a man, big, bearded, his skin burned almost black by the sun. He wore tattered buckskins and his hair was long and lank around his face. His eyes were open and glazed with pain and the front of his tunic was red and brown stained.

'Easy.' Rex let water trickle over the man's face. 'Take it easy.'

'Water!' The man clutched weakly at the canteen. 'Water!'

'Slowly now!' Rex let a little of the water trickle between the bearded lips. He waited a few minutes then gave the injured man a little more, knowing that too much water all at once could kill as surely as none at all. He followed the second draught with a little whiskey, then gave more water. The stimulant acted quickly. The man swallowed, licked his lips and tried to sit up. Rex restrained him, giving him another sip of the raw spirit.

'Should I go for help?' The preacher touched Rex on the arm. 'Maybe if I fetched a buckboard we could carry him to the ranch.'

'No.' Rex glanced down then walked out of earshot. 'He's dying,' he said, 'I can tell it from his wounds. Moving him would be a waste of time.'

'But we can't leave him here.' Toole glanced up at the setting sun. 'It will be dark soon and if he's helpless the buzzards and coyotes will come and tear him to pieces.'

'We won't leave him here alone,' Rex glanced back at the dying man. 'Collect some wood and light a fire. We'll camp here for to-night. If he's still alive in the morning you can ride back to the Circle Bar and have them send out the buckboard.'

'You think that is best?'

'I do.' Rex stared at the old preacher. 'You needn't stay if you don't want to. I can manage alone.'

'I'll stay.' Toole was firm. 'If that man

is dying then I may be able to bring him some comfort.'

'Yes,' said Rex. 'You may at that.' He turned and went back to the man while Toole collected the wood for a fire.

Together they sat by the comforting blaze waiting for the stranger to die.

8

Before the war Twin Forks had consisted of a couple of saloons, a thriving livery stable, hotel, feed store, gunsmith's and a row of shops and small businesses. It had promised to become the centre of trade and activity for the area but the war had put a check to its growth, Lamonte had sprung into greater importance as a stage terminal and, far from growing, the little township had shrunk.

Daren rode into town from the west sending his horse galloping along the single, main street, its hooves kicking up a plume of dust. He passed the Golden Eagle and halted at the clapboard building of the single lawyer, a pock-marked man named Junter. Hitching his horse to the rail he dusted himself down and stamped into the office, his spurs jingling as he walked.

'Wonder what Daren wants with Junter?' Stan Coleman, owner of the Golden Eagle, squinted through the window, then turned to Dancer. The gambler shrugged, expressing his usual indifference to what went on in the little town.

'Maybe he's gone to make a Will?' he suggested.

'A Will! Daren?' Coleman laughed as if the gambler had made the joke of the century. 'He don't need to make no Will.' Still laughing he led the way to the bar where he produced a bottle and glasses. 'Say when.'

'You say it.' Dancer took the brimming glass, lifted it to his lips and, with one quick gesture, tossed the raw spirit down his throat.

'Got a game going?' Coleman glanced to the room back of the bar where all the big money games took place.

'Not at the moment. Lintaker said he'd drop in later and I guess that Daren will want to try his luck.' Dancer hesitated, then decided against another

151

drink. 'Guess I'll get a little sunshine while I've the chance.'

'If you should see any of the Willards on the street duck for cover,' advised the saloon keeper. 'I heard tell that Daren's gunning for them. If they meet up the lead will be flying for sure.'

'I'll remember.' Dancer stepped out from the saloon and into the street. It was late afternoon and aside from a few old-timers sitting on the boardwalks the town seemed deserted. The depression had hit Twin Forks hard. The ranches couldn't afford to keep many cow-punchers and so little money found its way to the local businessmen.

The gambler took his time walking down the street. An alley ran beside the lawyer's office and he paused, took a cigar from his pocket and attempted to light it. A faint wind was blowing and he appeared to be having trouble. He looked up, glanced around, then stepped into the alley. If anyone was watching it would seem that he had merely stepped out of the wind. In reality he was doing something quite different.

Like all the buildings in Twin Forks, the lawyer's office was made of thin clapboard pegged to a wooden structure. The alley ran past it and into a back way where Junter stabled his horse. A lean-to contained feed, harness and a light wagon. A flimsy outbuilding held a copper and fuel for the fires. The place was deserted.

Moving, quickly and softly, Dancer slipped into the back premises and leaned his ear against the back wall. He heard a murmur of voices, frowned, then spotted a partly open window just above his head. Climbing on to the lean-to he crouched just beneath the window and the voices became clear and distinguishable.

'It isn't time yet.' Daren's voice held a cold finality. 'You do as I tell you, Junter, and don't get any ideas of your own. I put up the money, remember, and I get the gravy.'

'If we wait too long then the northern markets will boom and Leyburn will be able to meet his payments.' Junter had a peculiar whining voice, speaking through his nose most of the time. 'We've got to time it right, Daren, or we lose everything.'

'We'll lose nothing.' Daren was contemptuous. 'Let me handle this thing, Junter, as we agreed. You keep up the pressure and I'll talk Leyburn into widening his spread. The more he grabs the thinner his wallet will become. Good riders aren't easy to find and he'll need more than ordinary cowpokes to hold what he's after. He'll want topnotch gunmen and they don't come at no forty dollars a month.'

'So he'll keep spending until he's broke.' Junter sounded impatient. 'I know that, Daren, but I know something else too. The eastern syndicates are getting interested in ranching. A few of the big money men back east could put up a pile which would make what you loaned Leyburn look like chicken-feed. Suppose he sells out? He could take their money, pay off the note and leave us for a pair of suckers.'

'Not for long,' said Daren grimly. 'He tries anything like that and he'll be living in boot hill.'

'Can't you forget that gun of yours?' This time it was Junter who was contemptuous. 'Killing Leyburn won't put the Flying W in your pocket. All it will do is put a rope around your neck. Once he sells out then we can whistle for our money. We'll get what's due and not a cent more.'

'You're wrong,' said Daren.

'I'm not wrong. The trouble with you is that you think everything can be settled with a gun. So you loaned Leyburn ten thousand dollars. So you have his note and if he can't meet payment you'll own the ranch. All right. But you can't foreclose yet, and you won't be able to foreclose at all if he can meet the note when it's due. If he does we shall have doubled our money. Can't you be satisfied with that?'

'No.' Daren's heels hit the plank floor as he crossed the room and his voice sounded louder above Dancer's head. 'I put up the ten thousand and agreed to cut you in on half the profit or give you ten thousand, whichever was smaller. If I get the ranch you get the ten thousand. If Leyburn meets his note you get five and not a cent more. Isn't it worth going for the jackpot?'

'Five thousand maximum?' Junter laughed. 'I'm a cautious man, Daren, and I'm a lawyer. This thing has to be done legal if you ever want to own the Flying W. I say jump him now and take the lot.'

'We can't jump him now,' snapped Daren. 'What about the time limit on his note?'

'You should read the small type.' Junter chuckled. 'Cutting me in on the deal was the smartest thing you ever did, Daren. Clive don't know it but he's operating on sufferance. I sneaked in an option clause and we can take him up at any time we want. The only thing is the longer we leave it the more he'll have to pay. Compound interest, you know, or don't you care?'

'I care.' Again Daren's heels thudded the floor as he approached the window. 'But things are due to break, Junter, and break big. I've almost talked Clive into taking over the Circle Bar. When he does that and the gunsmoke's died away will be time enough to move in on his spread. He's registered his brand, remember, and registering all the extra range he's taken over as belonging to the Flying W. When he adds the Circle Bar he'll own the biggest spread in Texas.' He chuckled. 'Then we demand payment, he won't be able to meet it and then I'll own the biggest spread in Texas. Neat, eh?'

'If it works.' Junter made a sniffing noise. 'And what if the eastern syndicates decided to step in and make an offer?'

'They won't.'

'They may. They know that the markets will open up soon and they know that the ranchers are short of money. If they are going to buy at all now's the right time to do it. They can pick up a spread dirt cheap.'

'You've been giving this some thought, haven't you, Junter?' Daren's voice was suddenly cold. 'You thinking of crossing me?'

'What gives you that idea?'

'You did. You stand to make at the most a round ten thousand if our deal works out. Officially you hold Clive's note, only I know that you sold it to me for a dollar. If you wanted you could go behind my back, sell out to a syndicate and leave me holding the bag.' The foreman's voice became even colder. 'That is, of course, if you want to wake up dead one fine day.'

'You don't scare me, Daren.'

'Good. I don't take kindly to a man who scares easy.'

'But what you say makes sense.' Junter paused. 'How about making me a full partner?'

'Are you crazy? The Flying W will be worth maybe a million when Clive gets through with adding the Circle Bar.'

'I know.' Junter almost purred. 'A nice round sum a million dollars. Almost as nice a sum as that ten thousand you happened to have. In gold too, wasn't it. Mexican gold.'

'What are you driving at?' There was a soft click as of a cocked pistol.

'Shoot me Daren and some papers I've left with a friend will be sent to old man Willard.' Junter sounded as if he were sweating. 'Maybe he'd like to know how you came by that ten thousand just after John was found shot in the back.'

'You know?'

'I know.' Junter laughed and it wasn't pleasant laughter. 'I took a trip down into Mexico after you put up that money. I found the men you had bribed to tell that story to old man Willard. The cowpunchers told the truth all right, but they didn't know all of it, did they? They didn't know that you and Mark had been making a little money rustling Circle Bar and Flying W steers over the border. They didn't know either that Mark had arranged to steal that nine thousand dollars and split it with you later. You both were tired of ranch life and wanted to taste some adventure. But Mark was a boy, Daren, and you are a man. He trusted you but you knew better than to trust anyone.'

'Keep talking.' Daren sounded as though he were out of breath.

'So he lost at cards, not hard when you don't even try to win. He went to collect the gold, he had to have John with him before the clerk would hand it over. Outside the hotel he — What did he do, Daren? Stun John or shoot him? I'd say that he buffaloed him, then rode off to the hide-out. You came along, saw John lying stunned and took the opportunity to put a slug in his back. There was a hue and cry, you sloped off, found Mark and then? Did you kill him too, Daren?'

'I killed him.' Daren laughed. 'I gut-shot the fool and left him to die. You know why I did that? I wanted money, sure, but not to throw away in a saloon like Mark wanted to. I wanted the Flying W. For five years I've eaten dirt and let Leyburn ride me because I could afford to wait. Now I've got it, the Circle Bar too almost. Now I'm going to cash in and cash in big.'

'Sure, why not?' Junter coughed. 'That other thousand, Daren. Where did you get that? From your smuggling or from the trade with Lintaker?'

'You know a lot, don't you?' Daren moved to the window again. He stared out, looking towards the horizon, not seeing the gambler who crouched against the building.

'I know most of what goes on and what has gone on,' said Junter, 'Drop that gun, Daren!'

'What!' The foreman turned. 'Put down that derringer, you fool!'

'When you drop that Colt.' There was a click and a soft thud. 'That's better. Now let's be sensible about this. I know enough to get you hung and you know it.'

'Do you?' Daren was contemptuous.

'Don't you have to have proof?'

'I can get it if I have to. But proof doesn't matter. Once Leyburn knows that it is you, not I, who put up the money for his loan he will begin to suspect who killed his brother.'

'Let him. I'm not afraid of that soft fool!'

'Willard too will guess. Can you face him and his son, both?'

'I only wish I had the chance.'

'There speaks the gunman,' said Junter softly. 'All blind, bull-headed courage and no brains. So you think you can outgun them all? I tell you that Clive won't rest until you're dead. He'll hire a hundred owlhoots to settle you if he has to, but it won't come to that. You've got speed with a gun, Daren, but no man can avoid a bullet in the back. You'll be riding the trail one day, not thinking a thing and then, without warning, a Winchester will send a slug into your spine. Can you guard against that?'

Dancer didn't catch the reply. He

crouched against the building, a handkerchief to his mouth, fighting the
terrible desire to cough. He bit his lips
as he tried to control the spasm in his
lungs. He recovered in time to hear
Daren's voice.

'All right, Junter. Put away that gun
and let's not talk about killing each
other. The Flying W is a big enough
spread for us both. One third to you the
rest to me.'

'One third?'

'I put up the money, I'm taking the
risk and I'll take the most profit.'

'But only a third? I'm supplying the
brains, remember, and the legal know-
how. You wouldn't get far without me,
Daren.'

'I think different. I think that all your
talk of papers with a friend is bluff.' The
foreman's boots rapped on the floor
and furniture creaked as if beneath a
heavy weight. Daren, Dancer guessed,
was leaning on the desk.

'Get one thing straight, Junter. I
killed to get that money and killed to

hang on to it. One more dead man won't bother me none. It could be you or it could be Willard, or Clive or anyone who tries to stop me. Just don't get the idea that paper-talk and the law could stop me from putting lead in that fat stomach of yours if you tried to cross me. I'd shoot you down like the rat you are without a second thought. We're partners, yes, on my terms. But don't push me and don't get too smart. And I give the orders, remember that.'

Dancer felt fire stab his chest as he tensed beneath the window. The bout of coughing so long controlled could not be mastered any longer. Desperately he slipped from the lean-to and ran into the alley. Careless of whether he was seen or heard he doubled in a fit of coughing which temporarily blinded and deafened him to the world around him. When he finally straightened his handkerchief was spotted with bright red blood.

He wiped his lips and tucked the handkerchief in a pocket. He lit a cigar, feeling a strange satisfaction as the smoke hurt his chest. As usual the pain subsided and the tobacco smoke brought relief. Taking a deep breath the gambler looked around him.

Junter's office was as he had left it. No one had apparently heard him or, if they had, had guessed that he had been listening to the conversation between the lawyer and the foreman. It was just as well. Daren, Dancer knew, would have shot him down without a second's hesitation had he been discovered.

Slowly the gambler walked into the street and turned towards the Golden Eagle. What he had learned interested him. Daren, gunman though he might be, had hit on a sure method of getting rich. With the power his mortgage gave him over the Flying W his plans might well materialize and he knew, or guessed, that no eastern syndicate would be interested in buying into a range war. They would be interested when the beef began moving north to the waiting markets, when cattle now worth only three dollars a head would fetch twenty, thirty and even more when delivered to the buyers at the railhead.

As a gambler Dancer could appreciate the fine timing necessary and the clever balance Daren had struck between a small outlay of cash at the right moment and a potential fortune. Only Rex really stood in his way now, without the tall man the Circle Bar would revert to the Flying W. It was a shrewd, clever, well-thought-out scheme and Dancer could admire the concept if not the execution.

But Daren was dangerous in more ways than one. Junter had apparently forgotten that in his short-sighted greed. The gunman had been clever enough to plan his coup well ahead. Now the lawyer hoped to climb aboard the foreman's bandwagon and help himself to easy money.

Idly, Dancer wondered just how long the lawyer would live, then shook off the notion. He had more important things to worry about. He had to carry the news to Rex that his brother was dead and that Daren was the killer.

Turning into the Golden Eagle he called for a drink and sat down to wait. Rex could arrive that night, would arrive if the rumours circling the saloon had substance. Daren, apparently, had early signified his intention of challenging the tall man to a show-down. His arrival now meant that he had already sent word or at least expected to meet his rival. Rex, if he wanted to retain his pride, had to appear in town.

So Dancer waited while the sun lowered in the sky and night closed over the prairie. But Rex did not arrive.

Rex was waiting at the side of a dying man.

9

Dancer leaned back in his chair and sent a thin stream of smoke across the table. Opposite him, Lintaker, the Indian Agent, coughed and waved his hand before his face. Daren, a cigar in his mouth, looked up from his cards.

'I'll meet you, Coleman, and raise you fifty.'

'Too strong for me.' Lintaker threw down his hand and helped himself to a drink. Dancer said nothing but met the raise. Coleman called and cards were shown. Daren had three sevens, Coleman two pairs, Dancer took the pot with a low flush.

'You win again.' Daren scowled as he reached for the bottle. 'Hell, Dancer, no man should have such luck.'

'Want to quit?' Dancer knew what the answer would be. They had been playing since last night with a break for sleep and food and now it was getting toward noon. Daren had been losing and was in no mood to leave the game. He said so and the gambler shrugged.

'I'm waiting for that Rex Willard,' said Daren venomously. 'I'll wait until he shows up or until everyone knows him for the yellow coyote he is.'

'Won't Clive be expecting you back at the Flying W?' Coleman rolled his cigar around his mouth and looked at his cards. 'Pass.'

'Me too.' Lintaker eased his collar.

'To hell with Leyburn.' Daren tossed back his drink, wiped his mouth on the back of his hand and pushed some coins towards the centre of the table. 'Open for ten.'

'Make it twenty.' Dancer's white fingers pushed forward a double eagle. 'You say to hell with Leyburn, Daren, will you say it to his face?'

'Sure, why not?'

'Because he's just entered the saloon.' Dancer gestured towards the open door. Clive Leyburn hesitated in the main room of the saloon, saw the poker players and walked forward.

'Anyone seen Daren?' He grunted as he recognized the foreman. 'So here you are. I expected you back.'

'You was disappointed, weren't you?' Daren glanced up. 'I'm not going back to the ranch until I've settled with Willard. You may as well know that now as later.'

'There's plenty of work to be done.'

'The work can wait.' Daren glanced at Coleman. 'You staying or quitting?'

'Quitting.' The saloon owner threw down his hand. 'I've got work to do, boys, so I hope you'll excuse me. Want to take my place, Clive?'

'I don't know.' The boss of the Flying W hesitated, then accepted the vacant chair. 'Might as well, I guess. Someone's got to keep an eye on Daren.'

'You keep your nose out of this!' The foreman spoke with sudden viciousness. 'When I want you to hold my hand I'll let you know.' He stared at Lintaker. 'You playing or just sitting there?'

'Just sitting here, for this hand at least.' The Indian Agent threw down his cards.

Daren met the raise, drew two aces to the three tens he held and won a small pot. The victory seemed to cheer him.

'Luck's changing,' he said. 'Take a hand, Clive.'

Dancer dealt the cards without waiting for Leyburn to agree. Clive dug a handful of coins from his pocket and settled down to play. Dancer, his eyes veiled behind the smoke of his cigar, began to carry out a plan of his own.

As the play progressed the stakes began to mount higher. Daren won just often enough to make him eager for more.

Clive lost to both the gambler and to Lintaker. The play swayed back and forward until excitement had gripped the players and the pots began to mount higher and higher.

Daren was losing slowly, Clive faster and Lintaker just about held his own.

They had just finished a three-way

bluff with Dancer holding the edge when they were interrupted. Dan Willard, his old face seamed with worry, entered the back room with Curly at his side. Daren stiffened as he saw the old rancher.

'Hold it.' Curly lifted his hand and the light gleamed on the barrel of the Colt he carried. 'Reach for that iron, Daren, and I'll let you have it.'

'What is this!' Leyburn jerked to his feet. 'What's going on?'

'Where's Rex?' Dan stared from one face to the other. 'Tell me, where is he?'

'We haven't seen your son,' said Dancer quickly. 'He hasn't come into town.'

'Hasn't arrived?' Dan looked blank. 'He started out yesterday. You mean that you haven't seen him?'

'No.' Dancer stared at Curly. 'This is a quiet game of poker and we can do without guns. If you want to stay holster your iron.'

'Do as he says, Curly.' Dan sagged with a mixture of relief and worry. Rex hadn't yet met Daren and so far was safe from the foreman, but he should have arrived hours ago. He became aware of the gambler speaking to him.

'Sit down, Mr Willard, and take a hand. Rex will probably be along fairly soon.'

'He's yellow,' said Daren suddenly. 'He's like his old man, yellow right through.'

'Watch your tongue, Daren.' Dan stared at the foreman. 'No one calls me or mine a coward.'

'I'm saying it and saying it out loud.' Daren sneered. 'You needn't fear for your hide, old man, not if you've got sense. But that yellow son of yours is going to meet me or eat dirt.'

'We're playing cards,' said Dancer savagely. 'If you want to shoot off your mouth go out into the street.'

'You'll come with me?' Fury blazed in Daren's eyes as he stared at the gambler. 'You talk big, fancy man, can you back up your words?'

'I think so.' Dancer stared coldly at

the foreman. 'You don't scare me, Daren. I'm as good as dead already so a few more weeks can't make that much difference. Maybe you'll be doing me a favour if you shot me. But before you do it I'll get you. I swear it.' He began to shuffle the cards. 'You want to walk outside?'

Daren hesitated, chilled by something he didn't quite know. The gambler was a sick man and was probably careless of death. Once the foreman had seen a similar man fight a gun battle. He had been shot three times in the body but his spirit had overcome his wounds and he had killed the man who had challenged him. Against such fearlessness Daren was at a disadvantage. He relied on fear to weaken his opponents, to make their hand slow and clumsy so that their draw was delayed and their shots wild. Against a man filled with the determination to kill and without the fear of death he would be at a disadvantage. He shrugged and lit a fresh cigar.

'Deal the pasteboards, Dancer. I'll fight you with your own weapons.'

'Then you are a fool,' said the gambler softly. He looked at Dan. 'Sit in and join us, Mr Willard. I can guarantee a straight game. I have a feeling that this is one gamble the better man will win.'

Dan swallowed, glanced at Curly, then sat down. He knew the gambler to be a friend of his son and there had seemed to be an inner meaning to his words. Curly, sitting himself down beside his boss, relaxed and lit a quirley.

'Table stakes.' said Dancer and the pasteboards skimmed across the table. 'No holds barred and the sky's the limit.'

They settled down to the play.

Three hours later Dan had won almost all the money on the table. Lintaker, his last coin gone, had joined Curly in a watching brief. Daren, his forehead moist with perspiration, bit savagely on his cigar as he watched his pile of coins melt away. Leyburn looked physically ill as he scribbled another IOU.

'I hope that your paper is good, Clive,' said Dan evenly. He had not let the excitement of winning go to his head. Normally a cautious player, he found it hard to believe that he had held such consistently winning hands through sheer luck. His admiration for the gambler had grown as he saw how Dancer had cunningly swayed the play, bidding high and taking a pot himself when Dan had held poor cards. Bidding high to suck the money from the others when he had held good.

'It's good,' snapped Leyburn. 'The Flying W is worth all that and more.'

'The Flying W ain't what we're playing for,' said Daren suddenly.

'You said something?' Leyburn turned to his foreman. 'Maybe you're forgetting yourself, Daren. I pay your wages, remember that.'

Daren gritted his teeth at the insult, then his face hardened into a savage mask.

'I'm no hired hand,' he said. 'Better think twice before you get in too deep.'

'I should think that Clive's in too deep to back out now,' said Dancer evenly. 'How much does he owe you, Mr Willard?'

'Plenty.' Dan added up the IOUs. 'This paper is worth ten thousand dollars.' He shrugged. 'I guess it's worth just about what Confederate money is worth.'

'Watch what you say. Willard!' Leyburn went white with rage. 'That paper will be met.'

'When?' Dan was quick to take up the gambler's lead. 'You've got cattle, Leyburn, but so have I and we both know what cattle are worth. I've got land, and so have you but I didn't sit down to play for land. I stood to lose gold and I reckon that I should be paid in gold. You got it or are you playing on a bluff?'

'You'll answer for that, Willard!' Leyburn grabbed for the gun in his belt. Curly leaned forward and snatched it from its holster.

'No gunplay,' he said evenly. 'Not if you don't want me to join in. Dan's right in what he says. You've a big spread, Leyburn and you've money to pay your riders. If you ain't got money then why play at all? Seems to me that a man who plays for paper and who has nothing to back it is no more than a horse thief.'

'I've got the Flying W to back up my paper!' Leyburn snorted his contempt. 'It's worth five times that amount, and you know it!'

'It's worth what it will bring,' said Dan coldly. 'And that isn't much.'

'It's worth a damn sight more than the Circle Bar.'

'Now, gentlemen, let's remain calm about this.' Dancer leaned back, a smile on his lips. 'You say that the Flying W is worth more than the Circle Bar. All right. Would you say that it's worth the Circle Bar, the money on the table plus all your paper?'

'I don't know.' Leyburn looked at the

gambler. 'What are you getting at?'

'Your paper is worth ten thousand, that makes the Flying W worth that much less. The Circle Bar owns that ten thousand, that makes it worth just that much more. And Dan has three thousand in gold before him.' Dancer took a deliberate pull at his cigar. 'One against the other I'd say that they were even.' He hesitated. 'That is if both ranches are clear of debt. Are they?'

'The Circle Bar is,' said Willard. 'I don't know about the Flying W.'

'I — ' Leyburn hesitated, wetting his lips. 'That is — '

'If it's mortgaged then that alters the value,' said Dancer smoothly. 'Especially if it's the sort of mortgage which can be foreclosed at any time. Is it?'

'I'm in debt for ten thousand,' admitted Clive Leyburn. 'I'm safe so long as I can pay off the interest.' He looked down at the scattered cards. 'Why all the questions, anyway?'

'Just an idea,' said Dancer smoothly. 'Now suppose you were to play Dan for sole ownership of this part of the country? Winner take both ranches and what's on the table. Well?'

It was tempting and Leyburn hesitated. The heat of gambling had gripped him and he had lost more than he could afford. If he had to meet the IOUs and if the owner of his note were to press for payment he would be ruined. On the other hand, if he won back his paper, the money on the table and the Circle Bar, he would be the biggest cattle baron in Texas. He could sell out to an eastern syndicate and retire with a fortune. He could raise a loan to pay off the note without trouble. He could even sell his beef, the Circle Bar beef that is, at give-away prices and find the money that way. And he would still own the Flying W and the extra land.

Dan Willard sat and thought much the same thoughts. He was on the edge of ruin and had little hope of collecting the IOUs. By the turn of a card he could regain all that he had lost. If he won, that was, if he lost — He swallowed and stared at the gambler.

'One hand,' said Dancer. 'Cards dealt face up and the highest poker hand takes both spreads.'

'No.' Daren shook his head. 'No deal.'

'Stay out of this, Daren.' Clive turned towards the foreman. 'Keep your nose out of my business.'

'It is my business.' Anger and fear of the sudden collapse of his plan made the foreman desperate. 'You owe money and the man who loaned it to you has first call on the Flying W.'

'That man will be paid.' Leyburn stared hard at the foreman. 'We'll do it the gambler's way. We could win and if we do then we're in the chips. If we lose, then we're back where we started from.' He turned to the gambler. 'Deal the cards.'

'You can't do it!' Daren leapt to his feet white with rage. 'Damn you, Leyburn, you can't do it!'

'Sit down!' It was Curly and the Colt in his hand backed his words. 'Keep a

181

tight rein, Daren or get out. This is none of your business.'

'That's what you think. It's plenty my business.'

'How?'

'Yes, how, Daren?' Dancer smiled as his fingers shuffled the cards. 'You're just the foreman on the Flying W. How does this concern you?'

Almost too late Daren saw the trap. If he confessed that it had been he who had backed the loan then the inevitable question would be asked. Cowpunchers earned forty dollars a month and their keep. Foremen could earn up to twice that amount. He had been with Leyburn for five years and the man knew that he wasn't rich. That ten thousand could be accounted for only in one way. He swallowed.

'How?' urged Dancer. 'Tell us how?'

'Go to hell!' Daren reached over and snatched the cards. 'All right, so you want to risk the lot on one deal. That's your business. But I don't trust no fancy men.' He shuffled the cards, cut them, shuffled again and handed them to Curly. 'Split and mix them, we'll do this thing proper.'

Curly nodded, holstered his Colt and riffled the pasteboards. Dancer smiled and held out his hand for the pack. Curly placed them on the table and Dancer reached for them, then swore as steel flashed in the last rays of the dying sunlight. Daren had stabbed his knife directly through the pack and into the table.

'We'll pull them off the top,' he said grimly. 'No bottom dealing in this game. All right, fancy man, deal.'

Dancer swallowed. His careful plans seemed about to fall into ruin. All day he had nursed the play so as to reach this moment. The final deal, he knew, would have seen Dan sole owner of both spreads. He would have fixed that, had been fixing it when Daren had snatched the cards. He had tried to repair the damage at the very last, one shuffle and cut was all he needed to determine the winning hand. Daren's knife had put a stop to any subtle dealing. Now Dan would have to rely solely on the wheel of fortune. The deal would have to be honest.

'Deal,' repeated Daren. 'It's getting dark, let's get this thing over and done with.'

'Deal,' whispered Lintaker. He hunched forward, his eyes gleaming.

'Deal coming up. Leyburn first.' Dancer pulled a card from the pack, the knife making a ripping sound as it sliced through the pasteboard. 'Club King!' The ripped card landed face up before the boss of the Flying W.

'Heart ten!' Dan stared at his card.

'Club Jack!'

'Heart nine!'

'Diamond King!' Leyburn sucked in his breath as he stared at his pair of kings.

'Heart Jack.'

'Could be a flush,' whispered Curly. 'Or maybe a straight.'

'Club trey.' Dancer tossed down the card.

'Pair of kings,' said Lintaker. 'Maybe two pairs or three of a kind. Depends on the last card.'

'Shut your mouth,' snapped Daren. He craned forward as the fourth card fell before Dan.

'Heart seven.'

'A flush,' said Curly. 'Or a straight flush or maybe just a straight. Three chances, boss! Three winning chances!'

Dan nodded, his mouth dry. Slowly Dancer tore free Leyburn's last card.

'Club five.'

'Pair of kings,' said Lintaker. 'A fair enough hand. Looks like you take the pot, Clive.'

'Not yet he doesn't,' said Curly. 'The pot ain't won until the last card is down.'

'Quit your babbling,' snapped Daren. He sucked in his breath, perspiration glistening on his forehead. 'Deal.'

'Yes, deal, Dancer.' Lintaker leaned forward eagerly as the gambler stretched out his hand. 'What is it? Let's see who wins.'

Slowly the gambler touched the final card. For Dan to win it had to be any heart or the eight of any suit. Five hearts would give him a flush, an eight would give him a running sequence, a straight. Any other card and he would have lost the gamble. Tension in the room mounted as the gambler began to free the card. No one spoke, every eye was on the knife-stabbed pasteboards. Even breathing seemed to have been suspended.

'Heart four.' Dancer threw down the ripped pasteboard. 'Mr Willard gets a flush in hearts.'

'And a flush beats a pair of kings.' Curly jumped up and clapped Dan on the shoulder. 'You've won! By Satan, Dan, you've won!'

'No.' Leyburn stared at the cards, his face white and sagging. 'No.'

'What a game,' said Lintaker. 'High stakes, boys, that's what I like to see. A ranch won on the turn of a card.'

'No,' whispered Leyburn again. He felt sick, defeated, crushed by the sudden turn of fortune. In an instant he had been dashed from proud ownership of the Flying W to little more than a beggar. With the burden of defeat came a desperate attempt to deny what had happened.

'It was a frame. The gambler was working for the Circle Bar!'

'How was it a frame?' Curly was indignant. 'Your own ramrod shuffled the cards and speared them to the table. Those cards came off the top and you know it.' Understanding came to the cowpuncher. 'You trying to wriggle out of the deal, Leyburn?'

'He can't,' said Lintaker. 'It was a fair gamble.'

'It wasn't!' Clive looked at Daren. 'You know it wasn't. Damn it, Daren, are you going to stand by and see me robbed?'

'You fool!' Daren trembled with anger. 'You soft, blind fool! Don't come whining to me for help.'

'It was a frame!' Suddenly Leyburn lost his self-control. He had lost all he owned and he wanted to get it back. 'He cheated! The dealer cheated!' Abruptly his hand darted to his belt, snatched the Colt from its holster and began to level the weapon. Two shots sounded as one. The Colt fell to the floor and Leyburn looked foolishly down at his hand. It spurted blood from a wound in the wrist.

'Any other gentleman want to accuse me of cheating?' Dancer had not even moved but the derringer in his hand had two barrels and the men in the room knew that he wouldn't hesitate to use the remaining bullets in his hideaway gun.

'You didn't cheat,' said Curly, and swore to add emphasis. 'The deal was fair and I'll drill any man who says it wasn't.'

'It was fair,' said Lintaker.

'I won,' said Dan evenly. 'The Flying W is mine, Leyburn. I've got witnesses to the fact and I'll ask you to hand over the deeds.' He looked at Daren. 'As from now, Daren, you ain't working for the Flying W. Go and collect your gear. I want you out of the bunkhouse when I ride up to take possession.'

'You and who else?' Daren's hand flickered and his Colt menaced the room. 'Don't try it, Curly,' he warned. 'Don't any of you try anything.' He sucked in his breath. 'You don't own the Flying W, Willard. I do. I put up the money for Leyburn's note and I'm taking possession as from an hour ago.' The hammer of his Colt clicked back at full cock. 'And I'll kill any man tries to take it from me.'

'Then you'd better start killing, Daren.' Dan stared at the foreman. 'I'm giving you an hour and then I'm riding up to kick you out.'

'Maybe.' Daren circled the room and paused at the door. 'I ain't arguing with you, Willard, but if you set foot on the Flying W then I'll kill you. And the same goes for that son of yours. Tell him I'm tired of waiting. Tell him that he can find .me at the Flying W. Tell him that and watch him rub his belly in the dirt.'

He turned and left the room and the sound of his horse's hoofs drummed along the trail leading to the Flying W.

10

Rex arrived at the Golden Eagle as Dancer was dressing Leyburn's hand. He listened without comment as the gambler told him what had happened.

'So your father owns both spreads, Rex,' ended Dancer. 'He won them fair and legal no matter what this yellow-belly might say.' Dancer tied the last knot, helped himself to a drink and looked at the tall man. 'We expected you last night. What kept you?'

'I found a man dying on the prairie.' Rex looked hard at Lintaker. The Indian Agent had remained behind helping to drown his losses with Coleman's whiskey. He shrugged.

'So you found a man dying. Anyone we know?'

'I think so. He was a rustler. He recovered enough to be able to talk and when he found that Toole was a preacher he wanted to ease his mind. He told us all about how he rustled cattle, sold them to you at bottom prices so that you could supply the Indians with beef. The government make you an allowance so that the Indians get what they need. You robbed them of supplies and lined your own pockets. At the same time you were mixed up with rustlers.'

'You're crazy!' Lintaker reached for his bandanna and wiped his face.

'I'm not crazy,' said Rex. 'It all adds up. No one would search for their cattle on the reservation and if they did then the Indians would jump them. Stolen beef was safe enough once it had passed from your hands. It was butchered and the hides burned or buried. Just to make things even safer the brands were altered a little so as to give you an alibi.'

'Talk.' The agent seemed to regain his courage. 'Just talk.'

'No. The preacher wrote it all down and the dying man signed it. It's going to the Bureau of Indian Affairs,

Lintaker. I'll leave you to guess what happens next.'

'You're lying. Holman would never have done that.'

'Holman?' Rex took a long stride forward. 'How did you know who it was, Lintaker? I didn't mention his name. You knew it. How?'

'I — ' Lintaker wet his lips, then shrugged. 'So I knew his name. I caught him trying to sell rustled beef and we had an argument. He reached for his gun and I was faster on the draw. He ran for his horse and I let him go. He must have got weak, fell from his horse and lay where you found him. Simple.'

'Got it all worked out, haven't you?' Rex did not trouble to hide his contempt. 'You shot him all right and it was in an argument but it was over money you owed him, not over stolen cattle. But never mind Holman. Lopez is mixed up in it too.'

'A Mexican?' Dancer nodded, his face thoughtful. 'So that's how he got paid for his work. You covered yourself well, Lintaker, letting him win at poker. No one would guess that way.'

'I don't know what you're talking about,' said Lintaker, then began to bluster. 'So what if I have made a little money from the Indians? Am I the only one doing it? Indians ain't human anyway and the quicker they die off the better. You ain't got nothing on me but what Holman told you and who is going to believe what he said? You could have made it all up for what I know.'

'Yes,' said Rex evenly. 'That's right, isn't it?' Abruptly he was facing the other man. 'Listen to me, Lintaker,' he said. 'My father owns this part of the country and neither he nor I want to see you around. If you don't quit then I'm coming after you. If I see you on Circle Bar land I'm shooting first and asking questions afterwards. I don't like you or your type and I'm warning you now. Get moving. The next time we meet will be the last for one of us.'

He looked at the circle of faces staring at him as Lintaker stumbled from the saloon.

'Well? Where is Daren?'

'Daren's gone back to the Flying W,' said Dancer. 'He said that he's going to stick until someone can shift him.' He didn't look at Rex.

It was, the tall man thought, inevitable. Violence bred violence and no matter what he did he couldn't avoid death and the threat of death. It had started when he first rode home and now it had to be finished one way or the other. Daren had made his stand. He had to die or be allowed to do as he wished. He had flung down the gauntlet and Rex had to pick it up. Silently he left the room and headed for his horse.

It was a long ride to the Flying W. He didn't ride alone, Curly and Dancer were with him and Dan jogged silently at the rear. During the early stages of the journey they had talked, the gambler telling what he had overheard. It had come as no real surprise to either Dan or Rex to learn that Mark was dead. He had been wild, foolish, eager for excitement and chafing at responsibility, but he had deserved better than what Daren had given him.

'Does Clive know about this?' Rex had asked the question when the gambler had finished.

'No. I was figuring how to tell him when your father rode into town. I guessed that trouble was brewing and managed to get him into the game. I'd hoped to make Daren lose his head and he almost did.' The gambler made a small sound at the back of his throat, a sound which was strangled in a cough. 'Sure was a peculiar game.'

'Daren was smart,' said Curly. 'I was watching and my guess is that he made up his mind what he was going to do if the play went against him. I guess he thought that he had an even chance of winning.'

'He did,' said the gambler dryly. 'That last hand was one of the few honest deals in the entire game.'

'So now I own both spreads.' said Dan. He shook his head. 'Seems kind of rough on Clive though.'

'Why?' Rex was curt. 'He would have taken the Circle Bar had he won.'

'I know. But it still seems kind of rough.'

'A man gets what he gives. When he first met me I was a stranger to him, he didn't know me from Adam. Yet he threw his weight around as if I was dirt. He beat me up and left me to die. You think I should feel sorry for a man like that?'

'Maybe not.' Dan shook his head. 'Put like that I guess not.'

'This country can do without men like Leyburn,' said Rex. 'It has to do without them. We can't have cattle barons owning the land and deciding who should and who should not breathe their air. This is a free country and we want to keep it that way. Clive was tough when he was on top. He could afford to throw his weight around and trample others weaker than himself. Now he's got nothing and he can't expect the charity he refused to others.'

'And Daren?'

'Daren is as bad as Leyburn, maybe worse.'

'He's a sidewinder,' said Curly. 'He should be shot.'

'He will be,' said Rex, and after that they rode in silence.

It was late when they neared the buildings of the Flying W and yet late as it was the ranch showed signs of life. A fire blazed in the area before the house and men could be seen moving before the dancing flames. They were dressed and fully armed with rifles and pistols. Horses whinneyed from the corral. Rex halted his mount and leaned forward in his saddle.

'What's going on?' Dan drew his mount alongside that of his son. Curly and Dancer joined the pair, the gambler stifling a cough.

'Looks as though they were getting ready for us,' said Curly. 'Those rannies are armed with Winchesters and Colts and look as if they might be spoiling for trouble.' He glanced at

Rex. 'What you aim to do?'

'I'm going to do what I came here for,' said the tall man. 'This thing is between Daren and myself.'

'Looks as if he's turned out the Flying W,' said Dancer. 'There are a lot of gunhands riding for the ranch and Daren has them at his back. Maybe he's talked them into standing by him in his fight for the Flying W. From what I could see they regarded Daren as being their boss more than they ever did Leyburn.'

'We'll ride closer,' said Rex. 'I'll take the trail alone, you others ride to either side. If anyone starts shooting you can cover me.' He touched spurs to his mount and rode slowly forward. The others turned away from the trail and vanished into the gloom, only the soft thud of their horses' hoofs and the jingle of spurs and bridles showing where they rode. A man stepped forward as Rex rode into the firelight.

'Who goes?'

'Willard.' Rex reined in his horse.

'Daren sent me an invitation.'

'And you were fool enough to accept it.' The man grinned as he stared at the horseman. He was a tough cowpuncher who had handled more stolen beef than riding legitimate and his guns had earned him more money than he had ever collected by means of his rope.

'I've not come out here just to swap talk with Daren,' said Rex. 'I've come to take possession of the Flying W.' He stared towards the other men around the fire. They had grouped together and were looking towards him. Daren was not among them.

'We heard about that cheating deal,' said the cowpuncher. 'If you think you can take this ranch then you're welcome to try.' His hand dropped to the pistol at his waist. 'Maybe it won't be as easy as you think.'

'You're riding the wrong trail,' said Rex. 'That deal was open. Daren fixed the cards himself and it was a fair game. We won this spread and we're taking it. Maybe you can work for us, maybe not, but try anything and you won't be in any state to work for anyone but the Devil.'

'Big talk,' sneered the man. 'Maybe you'd like to back it with something more than words?'

'I didn't come here to argue with you,' said Rex coldly. 'Where's that sidewinder Daren?'

'Take your time.' The man grinned again. 'Step down and take it easy.'

Rex didn't move. His eyes searched the group of men standing just before the fire so that the leaping flames threw their shadows towards him. Tension was in the air and a cold hostility. These men, hard and tough as they were, would care nothing for the rights and wrongs of the card game. They rode for Daren and would back him in anything he chose to do.

'I came to see Daren,' Rex said coldly. 'I didn't think that he would want to hide himself behind his riders. From what I've heard he's fond of shooting off his mouth but now it seems that he's got a yellow streak a mile wide. Seems to me that a man who talks big should act big. Could be that Daren's afraid of backing his words without a gang of men behind him to back him up. Maybe you ought to go and change his socks for him, or tuck him in bed, or wipe his nose. Seems like he needs a few nursemaids.'

It was the right approach. He had diverted the men and made his visit a personal challenge to the foreman. They laughed, not at his crude attempt at humour but at the prospect of the foreman cutting him down in short order. And Daren would have to do it. Cowardice was the one thing these men would not tolerate. They would follow Daren to the gates of hell itself, they would back his land-grab with their guns and lives, but they would only follow a man they could respect. Daren's authority was based on fear. His reputation as a man fast on the draw and quick to kill held them where money or loyalty would not. But he had to maintain that reputation the hard way. Rex had challenged it, if the foreman failed to meet that challenge then his power would be lost.

'Well?' Rex sat easily on his horse. 'Where is the rattlesnake?'

'He's over in the ranch-house,' called a man. He stepped forward and Rex recognized Benson. 'You can step down, Rex, and welcome.'

'Thanks.' Rex slid his leg over the saddle-horn and dropped lightly to the ground. 'You aim to back his play, Benson?'

'I ride for my forty dollars a month,' said the cowpuncher. 'That ain't high enough for me to stick my neck out.' He hesitated, glancing at the others. 'You want I should fetch Daren?'

'Yes.' Benson was on his side, Rex knew, but the man dared not come out into the open just yet. Feeling was high against the Circle Bar and the balance could tip either way. If Daren killed Rex then the riders would mount and ride against the other ranch. There would be gunplay, killing and, when the smoke had died Daren would be firm in the saddle and in control of both spreads. He would stay that way for all who could oppose his claim would be dead. If that happened, Benson and all who now showed their sympathy to the Circle Bar would be treated as enemies.

But first Daren had to kill Rex.

And he had to do it in a special way. There was a code governing duels of this nature. It was man against man, nerve against nerve with victory going to the one who could walk away. Gunfights were usually at short range with both men facing each other, walking towards each other, bodies tense and hands trembling, over the butts of their guns. Then, when one of them decided the time was right, he would snatch at his weapon and blaze at his opponent. Either could draw first, there were no signals or any of the rules governing the duelling of the old world. It was draw and fire and kill if you could.

Tensely Rex waited for the foreman to appear.

He came after what seemed a long time, Benson walking behind and to one side. Daren was smiling, a cold, tiger smile of animal hate. He walked loosely, his hands at his sides, his body relaxed, Rex turned and faced him while behind him, the group of men faded out of the possible line of fire.

'You wanted to see me, Daren,' called Rex. 'Here I am.'

'You alone?' Daren paused, his cold eyes flickering as he stared into the darkness. 'I don't trust you, Willard, and I don't fancy collecting a rifle bullet in the back.'

'The only one who is going to shoot at you is me.' Rex felt his muscles tighten and forced them to relax. 'If you don't want to face me then you can ride off.'

'Scared?' Daren guessed by the offer that Rex was afraid to meet him. He spat and looked around him. The fire was behind the tall man and slightly to his right. It gave him a slight advantage as it illuminated the foreman but left him in darkness. Daren walked to his left so that the fire was between them. He did not make the mistake of easing his guns in their holsters, any such move would be the signal for the tall man to draw and fire. Instead he spat again, gauging the distance and his own capabilities.

The range was about thirty yards, near enough for accurate shooting. But Daren wanted to do more than just cut down the tall man, he wanted to impress his men. The longer he waited before reaching for his guns the better from that point of view. The more casual he appeared the greater would be their respect and fear. And he knew himself and had confidence that he could give Rex a head start and still win. Slowly he began to walk forward.

Rex waited a split second then moved forward in his turn. His reasoning was much the same as that of the foreman but he had added worries. He could kill

Daren and still have the others against him. He forced himself to ignore the possibility, concentrating solely on the matter at hand, trying to live from one moment to the next taking each in turn.

Daren was over-confident and thus inclined to be careless. He thought that he had already won and so was unworried. Against that he was a seasoned fighter and could trust his reflexes to take over when the need arose. His arm, hand and fingers would follow a regular pattern as he signalled his intention to draw. He would do it without conscious thought and so be that much faster. Rex took a deep breath and concentrated on the fore-man's right hand.

It was tense and curved, hovering a few inches above the gun butt. The left arm was also tense, the hand a little before the body ready to whip over and fan the hammer of the drawn Colt. Daren then used the fanning method to obtain rapid fire. Rex felt himself relax even more.

Fanning was sheer grandstand play and was derided by any really good gunfighter. It was successful against opponents unused to weapons, those slowed down by fear or those who were slow on the draw but it was useless against a man who was in full command of himself and who could school himself to obey the most essential rule in gunfighting, that of taking his time. Not much time, of course, a split second or so, but it could make all the difference between defeat and victory. A gun fanner could blast off five rapid shots and spray at his target with a blast of fire. But no gun fanner was or could be accurate. Colts weighed over three pounds and it was impossible to control the recoil when hammering at the gun with the edge of the left palm. The first shot might go home but the rest tended to go wild. A man who could force himself to take the time to aim accurately would have the advantage for his first shot would be the only one he needed.

'Scared, Willard?' Daren came closer, the firelight glinting from his eyes. 'Ever felt lead in the belly, Willard? I'll gut-shoot you the same as I did your brother and leave you to scream. Mark was yellow, Willard. He prayed that I wouldn't hurt him, whining like a yellow cur when he knew his chips were due. He — '

It was talk, but talk with a purpose. Daren hoped to make Rex mad with rage or weak with fear. At the least he hoped to distract him for a man listening to another will be that much off his guard. It could have worked, would have worked, but Rex didn't consciously hear a word the foreman said. He was looking at the foreman but he was seeing a fence post, the exact post he had shot at so many times, drawing and firing in a smooth, unthinking co-ordination of movement. Only this post had a hand and the signal to reach for his gun would he when that hand moved.

Daren went for his gun.

It was quick, incredibly quick, the hand seeming to blur as it dropped, lifted and levelled the Colt. The left hand swung and dropped, the edge hitting the hammer and fire and smoke spouted from the long, gleaming barrel. Something hit against the top of Rex's shoulder, tugging at him as if he had received a blow then his gun fired twice and the fence post that was Daren swayed, looked foolish, and toppled, a hole showing black between the eyes.

'He's dead! Daren's dead!' a man yelled, then swore with sudden anger. 'Get him, boys!'

'Hold it!' Rex swung, the gun in his hand staring at the men with its single, hungry eye. 'I'll get the first man who goes for a gun.'

'Like hell he will!' The speaker was the man who had met Rex when he rode towards the ranch. 'He can't get all of us, can he? You going to let — '

He choked and spun, blood gushing from his mouth as he crumpled to the ground and the sharp, spiteful crack of a rifle echoed through the night. A second gun fired, a third, then all four together, the bullets droning like hornets as they hummed above the heads of the men. Another burst scattered the embers of the fire, sending up a shower of sparks which danced and died as they fell to earth.

'Hold it, you rannies,' yelled Curly from the darkness. 'Just unbuckle those guns and let them drop. Easy now or you'll collect lead.' He rode forward into the firelight, his rifle slanted over his saddle. 'That's the idea, now step away from that hardware, get your horses and vamoose away from here.'

'All of us?' Lem, looking pale and scared in the firelight looked at the cowpuncher.

'You heard what I said.'

'Wait a minute,' Rex motioned to Benson. He lowered his voice as the cowpuncher joined him. 'You know these men and who are gunhands and who are good riders. Pick out the riders and move them to one side. Leave the gunhands Daren hired to do his dirty work. They go, the rest of you can stay if you don't mind working for the Circle Bar.'

'That'd be about half,' said Benson. 'I figure that they'd rather work for the Circle Bar than ride for Daren. Leastways they would have done if he'd still been alive.'

'Check and make sure. Arm the men you can trust and put the others into the bunkhouse. Come dawn you escort them off the Flying W and Circle Bar.'

'Leave it with me.' Benson walked away and joined the group. He spoke to several men who stared towards Rex, looked at Benson, then went to collect their guns. Curly hefted his rifle as they came close.

'It's all right, Curly,' Rex explained what was happening. 'We don't want to turn those gunhands out in the dark so as to cause trouble.' Rex winced at a sudden stab of pain from his wounded shoulder. 'Where are the rest?'

'Out standing by.' Curly jerked his

head towards the darkness. 'We figured that you might be wanting some help so took cover. Had they tried to jump you we would have opened fire. Couldn't do much against Daren though.' He sounded apologetic but Rex knew he spoke the simple truth. He had had to face the foreman alone. He looked up as his father came riding towards him, the gambler at his side.

'Rex! You're hurt!'

'Only a minor wound.' Dancer had dismounted and examined the tall man's shoulder. 'No bones broken and it's clean.' He whipped a clean handkerchief out of his pocket and made a swab to staunch the blood. 'He'll be all right in a few days.'

'So it's over,' Dan tipped back his hat and stared around at the ranch buildings. 'You know, I still can't believe that all this is mine.'

'It's yours all right,' said Curly.

'You won it fair,' said the gambler, and winked at Rex. The tall man smiled.

'I know you fixed some of the deals,'

said Dan quietly. 'But that last deal no one could have fixed. That is why I'm taking what I won. It was a fair gamble, But I feel that I owe you something, Dancer, probably more than I can ever repay.'

'You owe me nothing,' replied the gambler. 'Nothing at all.'

'So you say. But the Circle Bar is your home whenever you want it. And if there's ever anything else you want, money, men to back you in an argument, anything, just let me know what it is.'

'I'll remember that.' Dancer didn't press the subject, he knew that the old man meant exactly what he had said. 'A pity about your brother,' he said to Rex. 'Married, too, wasn't he?'

'Yes.'

'Someone ought to tell his wife. Want me to do it?'

'I'll tell her.' Rex eased his wounded shoulder. 'I'll ride over and tell her now.'

'Sure,' said Dan. 'But, Rex.'

'Yes?'

'Don't make the same mistake you made six years ago, son.'

'No,' said Rex. 'I won't do that.'

He was smiling as he rode into the night.

THE END

Other titles in the
Linford Western Library:

THE BLOOD RUNS DEEP

Peter Taylor

Jim and Aaron were brothers. Jim was dark-skinned and Aaron was white, and this created a chasm between them that widened when Jim ran off to fight in the Civil War. After the war, and fleeing from the army and hostile Comanches, Jim rides into Texas seeking his mother. But soon the two brothers are united in pursuit of renegades and Red Bill, an adversary from Jim's war days . . . Jim and Aaron's relationship is tested. Does their shared blood count?

DEAD MAN'S BOOTS

Edwin Derek

A posse is on the trail of outlaw Jack Crow when he discovers the body of a Texas Ranger. He assumes the dead man's identity and evades his pursuers. Now, accepted as a ranger, he upholds the law: siding with homesteaders in a range war against a gang of gun-runners and the Lazy Creek ranch. In a final showdown with the renegade gang leader, Jack discovers that a dead man's boots are harder to take off than put on . . .

Contents

Black Beauty

ANNA SEWELL

Level 2

Retold by John Davage

Series Editors: Andy Hopkins and Jocelyn Potter

Pearson Education Limited
Edinburgh Gate, Harlow,
Essex CM20 2JE, England
and Associated Companies throughout the world.

ISBN 0 582 42121 7

This edition first published 2000

NEW EDITION

Second impression 2001
Copyright © Penguin Books Ltd 2000
Illustrations by Victor Ambrus
Cover design by Bender Richardson White

Typeset by Pantek Arts Ltd, Maidstone, Kent
Set in 11/14pt Bembo
Printed in Denmark by Norhaven A/S, Viborg

Published by Pearson Education Limited in association with
Penguin Books Ltd, both companies being subsidiaries of Pearson Plc

For a complete list of the titles available in the Penguin Readers series please write to your local
Pearson Education office or to: Marketing Department, Penguin Longman Publishing,
5 Bentinck Street, London, W1M 5RN.

Introduction

'Always be good, so people will love you. Always work hard and do your best.'

These were the words of Black Beauty's mother to her son when he was only a young horse. At that time, they lived with Farmer Grey. But when Black Beauty got older, this was sometimes very difficult for him. Not everybody was as kind as Farmer Grey.

Anna Sewell was born in Great Yarmouth, in Norfolk, England, in 1820. She had an accident when she was about fourteen years old. After this she could not walk without help. *Black Beauty* was her only book. She wrote it because she loved horses. It hurt her when somebody was unkind to a horse.

There were no cars or buses in those days. There were trains between the towns and cities. In town or in the country you walked, or used a horse. The horse carried you, or pulled you in a carriage, cart or bus. It brought milk, bread and other things to your house.

There were many thousands of horses at work in Europe, America and other countries. Some worked for good, kind people, but some did not. Often the animals had to pull very heavy things, and they had to work for hours and hours. Anna Sewell knew this, and she wanted to tell other people. So she wrote her book.

She was often ill, and in 1871 a doctor told her mother, 'Anna has only eighteen months now.' Soon after this, Anna started writing her book. She finished it in 1877 and died in 1878, only a year after *Black Beauty* went into the bookshops. But many people were kinder to horses after they read Anna's book.

Chapter 1   My Mother

I don't remember everything about the first months of my life. I remember a big field of green grass with one or two trees in it. On hot days my mother stood under a tree and I drank her milk. That was before I got bigger. Then I started to eat the grass.

There were other young horses in the field. We ran and jumped round and round the field. We fell on our backs in the grass and kicked our legs happily.

When I stopped drinking her milk, my mother went to work every day. Then, in the evening, I told her about my day.

'I'm happy because *you* are happy,' she said. 'But remember – you aren't the same as these other young horses. They are going to be farm horses. They're good horses, but we are different. People know your father, and *my* father was Lord Westland's best horse. When you're older, you'll learn to carry people on your back. Or you'll take them from place to place in their carriages.'

'Is that your work, Mother?' I asked. 'Do you do that for Farmer Grey?'

'Yes,' said my mother. 'Farmer Grey sometimes rides me, and sometimes I pull his carriage. Here he is now.'

Farmer Grey came into the field. He was a good, kind man, and he liked my mother.

'Well, my dear,' he said to her, ' here's something for you.' He gave her some sugar. 'And how is your little son?' He put a hand on my back and gave me some bread. It was very nice.

We couldn't answer him. He put a hand on my mother's back, then he went away.

'He's very kind,' my mother said. 'Always do your work happily. Never bite or kick. Then he'll always be nice to you.'

1

We ran and jumped round and round the field.

Chapter 2   Lessons

I got older and my coat started to shine. It was black, but I had one white foot, a white star on my face and some white on my back.

When I was a big horse, Mr Gordon came to me. He looked at my eyes, my mouth and my legs.

'Very good,' he said. 'Very good. Now he'll have to learn to work. He'll be a very good horse then.'

What does a horse have to learn?

He learns not to move when a man puts a harness on him. Or when the man puts a bit into his mouth. A bit is a cold, hard thing, and it hurts. You can't move it. It stays in your mouth because the head harness goes over your head, under your mouth and across your nose.

I wasn't happy with the bit in my mouth, but Farmer Grey was a kind man in every other way. I didn't bite or kick. My mother always had a bit in her mouth when she worked. Other horses have bits too, and I knew that. So I didn't move when they put it in. Soon it didn't hurt.

The saddle wasn't as bad as the bit. Horses have to learn to have a saddle, and to carry a man, woman, or child on their backs. They have to walk, or to go a little faster. Or to go very fast.

They put the bit in my mouth and the saddle on my back every day. Then Farmer Grey walked with me round the big field. After that, he gave me some good food and spoke to me. I liked the food and the kind words. I wasn't afraid now of the bit and the saddle.

One day Farmer Grey got on my back and sat there in the saddle. The next day he rode me round the field. It wasn't very nice with a man in the saddle, but I was happy with my kind farmer on my back. He rode me in the field every day after that.

The next bad thing were the shoes for my feet. These, too, were cold and hard. A man put them on me. Farmer Grey went

3

with me, but I was afraid. The man took my feet in his hands. Then he cut away some of the hard foot. It didn't hurt me. I stood on three legs when he did the other foot. Then the man made shoes for my feet.

It didn't hurt when he put them on. But I couldn't move my feet easily. But later I started to like the shoes, and the hard roads didn't hurt my feet.

Next I learned to go in carriage harness. There was a very small saddle, but there was a big collar.

Farmer Grey told me to pull a carriage with my mother. 'You'll learn a lot from her,' he said, when he put the harness on me.

I did learn. She showed me the way to move, and she taught me to listen to the driver.

'But there are good drivers and bad drivers,' she said. 'And there are good people and bad people. Farmer Grey is kind, and he thinks about his horses. But some men are bad, or stupid. Always be good, so people will love you. Always work hard and do your best.'

Chapter 3   Birtwick Park

In May a man came and took me away to Mr Gordon's home at Birtwick Park.

'Be a good horse,' Farmer Grey said to me, 'and work hard.'

I couldn't say anything, so I put my nose in his hand. He put a hand on my back and smiled kindly.

Birtwick Park was big. There was a large house. And there were a lot of stables for horses, and places for many carriages. I went to a stable for four horses.

They gave me some food, and then I looked round. There was a horse near me in the stable. He was small and fat, with a pretty head and happy eyes.

'My name is Merrylegs. I'm very beautiful.'

'Who are you?' I asked.

'My name is Merrylegs,' he said. 'I'm very beautiful. I carry the girls on my back. Everybody loves me. You are living in this stable with me, so you will have to be good now. I hope you don't bite.'

A horse looked at Merrylegs from across the stable. She had a very beautiful red-brown coat, but she had angry eyes. She put her ears back.

'Did I bite you?' she asked angrily.

'No, no!' Merrylegs said quickly.

When the red-brown horse went out to work that afternoon, Merrylegs told me about her.

'Ginger does bite,' he said. 'One day she bit James in the arm and hurt him. Miss Flora and Miss Jessie, Mr Gordon's little girls, are afraid of her. They don't bring me nice food now, because Ginger is here.'

'Why does she bite?' I asked. 'Is she bad?'

'Oh, no! I think she was very unhappy. She says, "Nobody was kind to me before I came here." She'll change here. I'm twelve years old, and I know about life. There isn't a better place for a horse than this, anywhere. John is the best groom in the country and James is the kindest boy. Mr Gordon is a very nice man. Yes, Ginger will change here.'

Chapter 4   I Begin Well

The head groom's name was John Manly. He lived with his wife and one little child in a very small house near the stables.

The next morning he took me outside the stable and groomed me. He worked hard, and he made my coat clean and beautiful. Then Mr Gordon came and looked at me.

'He looks very good,' he said. 'I wanted to try him this morning, but I have some other work. You ride him, John, and then tell me about him.'

John put a saddle on my back, but it was too small. He changed it. He got another saddle, not too big and not too small, and we went out. He was a very good rider and I understood his words. On the road we walked, then we went faster. I wanted him to like riding me. Then he took me away from the road to some open fields with one or two trees and a lot of grass. There he wanted me to go very fast, and I did. It was good — I liked it! I think John liked it, too.

When we were at Birtwick Park again, Mr Gordon asked John Manly, 'Well, John, how does he go?'

'He's very good — very good,' said John. 'He loves going fast. He understands you. Nobody was unkind to him when he was young. So he isn't afraid of anybody or anything.'

'Good,' Mr Gordon said. 'I'll ride him tomorrow.'

◆

The next day, John groomed me and put the saddle on me. Then he took me from the stables to the house.

I remembered my mother's words and I tried to make Mr Gordon happy with me. He was a very good rider, and he was kind to me.

His wife was at the door of the big house when he finished riding. 'Well, my dear,' she said, 'how do you like him?'

'He's black and very beautiful,' said Mr Gordon. 'What can we call him?'

'We can call him Black Beauty!' said his wife.

'Black Beauty — yes — yes,' said Mr Gordon. 'I think that's a very good name.'

John came and took me to the stables.

'We've got a name for him, John,' said Mr Gordon. 'My wife thought of it. He's going to be Black Beauty.'

John was very happy. 'Come with me, my Black Beauty,' he said. 'You *are* a beauty — and it's a good English name.'

Chapter 5 My New Friends

John liked me. He was a very good groom, and my black coat always shone beautifully. He looked at my feet every day. He knew when one of them hurt. Then he put something on to it. He often talked to me. I didn't know every word, but I soon understood him. I liked John Manly more than anybody.

I liked the stable boy, James Howard, too. John taught him to be kind to horses, and he helped John to groom me.

After two or three days, I pulled a carriage with Ginger. I was afraid of her. She put her ears back when they took me across to her. But she didn't move when they harnessed me next to her.

John drove us, and we worked very well. Ginger worked well. She pulled as hard as me, and she also liked going more quickly. Many horses only go fast when the driver hits them with his whip. Ginger and I went fast when the driver wanted us to go fast. We went as fast as we could. John didn't like the whip, and he never whipped us. We worked hard for him.

After Ginger and I went out two or three times with the carriage, we were good friends.

We liked little Merrylegs very much. He was never afraid and always happy. Mr Gordon's little girls loved riding him, and they were never afraid. Mrs Gordon loved all three of us, and we loved her.

Mr Gordon liked his people to have one day without work every week. His horses also had a day without work. On Sunday they took us to a field of good grass, and we stayed there all day, without reins or harness. We ran and jumped. We played, and we were happy. Then we stood under some trees and told stories.

Chapter 6   James Howard

Mr Gordon came to the stables one day and spoke to John Manly. 'How is James working, John?' he asked.

'Very well,' John answered. 'He learns quickly. He is kind to the horses, and the horses like him. He's learning to drive, and he'll soon be a good driver.'

Then James came in. 'James,' Mr Gordon said. 'I have a letter from my friend, Sir Clifford Williams of Clifford Hall. He wants to find a good young groom. He pays well, and the young man will soon be head groom. He will have a room, stable clothes and driving clothes, and boys will help him. I don't want to lose you, and John will be sad.'

'I will. Yes, I will,' John said. 'But I won't try to stop him.'

'Yes, we'll all be sad,' Mr Gordon said. 'But we want you to do well, James. Do you want to go? Speak to your mother at dinner-time, James, and then give me your answer. Then I can tell Sir Clifford.'

Ginger and Merrylegs and I were sad, too, when we heard James's answer. He wanted to go. But it was a better job for him. We knew that.

For six weeks before James went, we worked hard. He wanted to be a very good driver, and Mr Gordon and John Manly wanted to help him.

So the carriage went out every day. Ginger and I pulled it, and James drove. James learnt very quickly. For the first three weeks John sat next to him, but after that James drove without him.

One day in autumn, after two or three days of heavy rain, Mr Gordon wanted John to take him to the city. There was a strong wind that day.

We came to the river. The water was very high under the bridge, and there was water across the fields.

We arrived without a problem. But it was late in the afternoon before we started for home again.

9

The wind was stronger now, and it made a noise in the trees. Suddenly, one of the trees fell across the road with a CRASH!

I was afraid, but I didn't run away. John jumped out of the carriage and came to me.

'We can't go past the tree,' John said to Mr Gordon. 'We'll have to go on the other road to the bridge. It's a longer road and we'll be late. But the horse isn't tired.'

It was nearly dark when we arrived at the bridge. We could see water on it. This sometimes happened when the river was high.

I started to walk across the bridge – but I stopped. Something was wrong. I could feel it.

'Move, Beauty!' said Mr Gordon.

I didn't move, and he put the whip across my back.

'Go now!' he said.

But I didn't go.

'There's a problem,' said John. He jumped down from the carriage and tried to move me. 'What's the problem, Beauty?' he asked.

There was a house across the bridge, and a man ran out of the door. 'Stop! Stop!' he shouted. 'The bridge is breaking in the middle. Don't come across it, or you'll fall in the river!'

John looked at me and smiled. 'Thank you, Beauty,' he said.

We went home on a different road. It was late when we got home. Mrs Gordon ran out of the house.

'You're late!' she said. 'Did you have an accident?'

'We nearly did,' said her husband. 'But Beauty is cleverer than us!'

◆

'I have to go to the city again,' Mr Gordon often said. And we always went when there were a lot of carriages and riders on the road. People were on their way to the train, or they were on their way home across the bridge after work.

Then one day Mr Gordon said to John Manly, 'Mrs Gordon and I have to go to Oxford tomorrow. We'll have Ginger and Black Beauty with the big carriage, and James will drive us.'

It was a journey of about seventy-five kilometres to Oxford. We went about fifty kilometres in one day and then we stopped for the night at the biggest hotel in Aylesbury. James drove very well. We pulled the carriage up and down, and he always stopped on the way up. He never drove us fast when we went down. We had to go quickly when the road was good, but not on bad roads. These things help a horse. And when he gets kind words, too, he is happy.

They groomed us in the hotel stable, and gave us some good food. James said, 'Good night, my beauties. Sleep well, Ginger. Sleep well, Black Beauty.' Then he went to his bed.

Chapter 7   The Fire

An hour later, a man came to the hotel on a horse. One of the hotel grooms brought the horse to the stable.

At Birtwick Park nobody smoked in the stables, but this man did. There was no food in the stable for the new horse, so the groom went to get some. The food for the horses was on the floor above the stable. The groom went up there and found some food. He threw it on the floor for the horse, and he went away.

I slept, but I soon woke up again. I was very unhappy. But why? I didn't know.

I heard Ginger. She was unhappy, too.

Then I saw the smoke.

Very soon there was smoke everywhere. There were noises from above my head – the sounds of a fire. The other horses in the stable woke up. They moved their feet and tried to get away from the smoke.

I was very afraid.

Then the hotel groom came into the stable and tried to take the horses out. But he was afraid, too, and he tried to work quickly. That made us more afraid, and the other horses didn't want to go with him. When he came to me, he tried to pull me out fast. He pulled and pulled. I couldn't go with him.

We were stupid – yes! But we didn't know him, and he was very afraid.

There was more and more smoke. And then we saw the red light of fire from the floor above our heads. Somebody shouted 'Fire!' outside, and more men came into the stable.

The sound of the fire was louder and louder. And then – James was at my head. He spoke to me quietly: 'Come, my beauty. We have to go now. Wake up and come with me. We'll soon get out of this smoke.'

He put a coat round my head and over my eyes. Then I couldn't see the fire, and I wasn't afraid. He spoke to me kindly and we walked out of the stable.

'Here, somebody,' James called. 'Take this horse, and I'll go back for the other horse.'

A big man took me, and James ran into the stable again. I was very unhappy when I saw him do this. I made a lot of noise. (Next day, Ginger said, 'When I heard you, I wasn't afraid. So I came out with James.')

A lot of things happened all round me, but I watched the stable door. There was fire and smoke inside, and things fell to the ground.

Mr Gordon ran to the stable. 'James! James Howard!' he called. 'Are you there?' There was no answer, but I heard more noises in the stable. Other things fell from the top floor. I was very afraid for James and Ginger.

I was happy when James and Ginger came out through the smoke to us.

He spoke to me kindly and we walked out of the stable.

'Good boy!' Mr Gordon said to James. 'Are you all right?'

James couldn't speak because of the smoke, but he was fine. He put a hand on Ginger's head and looked happy.

Chapter 8   Little Joe Green

James and Ginger were ill the next day. The smoke was bad for them. So we stayed in Aylesbury for that day. But after another night there, they were better. In the morning we went to Oxford.

James did everything for Ginger. He spoke to older grooms and they told him the best ways. When we arrived home at Birtwick Park, we were all fine.

John heard James Howard's story, and he looked at Ginger and me.

'You did well, James,' he said. 'A lot of people can't get horses out of a stable when there's a fire. Why don't they want to move? Nobody knows. Only a friend can take them out. They have to know and love him.'

Before he left us for his new job, James asked, 'Who's going to do my job? Do you know?'

'Yes,' John said. 'Little Joe Green.'

'Little Joe Green!' said James. 'He's only a child!'

'He's fourteen,' John said.

'But he's very small,' said James.

'Yes, he's small, but he's quick,' said John. 'And he wants to learn, and he's kind. His father will be happy, and Mr Gordon wants to have him here.'

James wasn't very happy about it. 'He's a good boy,' he said. 'But you'll have a lot of work because he's small.'

'Well,' John said, 'work and I are good friends. I'm not afraid of work.'

'I know that,' said James. 'And I'll try hard to be the same.'

The next day, Joe came to the stables. James wanted to teach him before he went. Joe learnt to clean the stable, and to bring in our food. He cleaned the harnesses, and helped to wash the carriages. He couldn't groom Ginger or me because he was too small. So James helped him groom Merrylegs.

Merrylegs wasn't very happy. 'The boy knows nothing,' he said. But after a week or two he said, 'I think the boy will be good. I'll help him to learn quickly.'

Little Joe Green was a happy boy. He sang when he worked. We soon liked him.

Chapter 9   I am Ill

One night, after James went away, I heard John outside. He ran to the house, then he ran to the stable. He opened the door and came to me.

'Wake up, Beauty!' he said. 'You have to run now!'

He put a saddle on me very quickly, and he jumped on my back. Then he rode me quickly to the house. Mr Gordon was there, with a light in his hand.

'Now, John,' he said, 'you have to ride as fast as you can. My wife is very ill. Give this letter to Doctor White in Hertford. I want him to come quickly. You can come home when Black Beauty is ready for the journey.'

John took the letter, and we went away.

'Now, Beauty,' said John. 'Do your best!'

It was night, but I knew the road. There were no people on it because they were all in bed and asleep. I went very fast – faster than every journey before that night.

When we came to the bridge, John pulled the reins. I went across it more slowly.

'Good, Beauty!' he said.

When we were across it, I went fast again. We went up and down, past fields and houses, and then through the streets of Hertford.

My shoes made a noise on the road when I stopped at the doctor's door. It was three o'clock in the morning. The doctor's window opened, and Doctor White looked out of it.

'What do you want?' he asked.

'Mrs Gordon is very ill,' John told him. 'Mr Gordon wants you to go quickly, or she'll die. Here's a letter from him.'

'I'll come down,' said the doctor. He shut the window and he was soon at the door. He read the letter. 'Yes,' he said, 'I'll have to go. But my old horse was out all day, and he's very tired now. My other horse is ill. What can I do? Can I have your horse?'

'He ran fast on the way here,' John said. 'But I think he can take you.'

'I'll be ready soon,' the doctor said, and he went into the house again.

John stood next to me and put his hand on my head. I was very hot.

The doctor came out in his riding clothes and with a riding whip.

'You won't want a whip,' John said. 'Black Beauty will go as fast as he can.'

'Thank you,' the doctor said. He gave the whip to John and spoke to me: 'Now, Black Beauty!'

The doctor was a bigger man than John, and he wasn't a very good rider. But I ran for him.

I was very tired, but we arrived at Birtwick Park very quickly. Then I nearly fell down. Mr Gordon heard us. He ran to the door and took the doctor into the house.

Little Joe Green was outside the door, and he took me to the stable. I was happy now, but I was very, very hot. My coat was hot, and water ran down my legs.

Joe was young and very small, but he tried. He cleaned my legs and my back, but he didn't put anything over me. He thought, 'The horse is hot and he won't like it.' He brought me a lot of water. It was cold and very nice, and I drank it. Then he gave me some food.

'Now sleep, Beauty,' he said, and he went away.

Soon I started to feel cold and ill. I tried to sleep, but I couldn't.

I was very ill when John came. He walked from Hertford, but he came to me. I was on the floor.

'Oh, Beauty!' he said. 'What did we do to you?'

I couldn't tell him, but he knew. He put things over me and made me warm. Then he ran to his house and brought hot water. He made a good drink for me. He was angry.

I heard him with the other men. 'A stupid boy!' he said. 'A stupid boy! He puts nothing on a hot horse! He gives him cold water! Oh, Beauty!'

I was very ill for a week. John was with me for hours every day, and he came to me two or three times every night. Mr Gordon came every day, too.

'Dear Beauty,' he said one day. 'My good horse! My wife didn't die, and we can thank you for that! Yes, we have to thank you!'

I was very happy about that. We all loved Mrs Gordon. Doctor White came one day when he was at Birtwick Park. He put a hand on my head and told John, 'Mrs Gordon is here today because this beautiful horse brought me here quickly.'

John said to Mr Gordon, 'Black Beauty went very fast that night. Do you think that he knew?'

I did know. John and I had to go fast for dear Mrs Gordon. I knew that very well.

Chapter 10   I Move Again

I was happy at Birtwick Park for another year. Only one thing made us sad: Mrs Gordon got better, but she was often ill again.

Then the doctor said, 'You and your wife have to go away and live in the south of France, Mr Gordon.'

'We'll go,' said Mr Gordon. 'We'll make a new home there.'

We were very sad. Mr Gordon was unhappy, too, but he started to get ready. We heard a lot of talk about it in the stable. John was very sad. Joe nearly stopped singing when he worked.

Mr Gordon's little girls came to the stable. They visited Merrylegs for the last time. They cried, but they told Merrylegs: 'You'll be happy, old friend. Father is giving you to Mr Good, the kind old church man. You'll take his wife from place to place, but you will never work hard. Joe will go with you. He's going to be the groom and he's going to help in their house next to the church. You'll see your friends Black Beauty and Ginger sometimes. Father is selling them to Lord Westland at Earls Hall. That isn't a long way.'

Mr Gordon wanted to find a job for John, too. But John wanted to open a school and teach young horses their work.

'A lot of young horses are afraid when they learn new things,' he said. 'Horses are my friends, and they like me. I think they'll learn better from a kind person. I want to teach them.'

'Nobody can do it better than you, John,' Mr Gordon said. 'Horses love you. And I'm very sad because I won't see you.'

The last day came. Ginger and I took the carriage to the door of the house for the last time. People came to the door when Mr Gordon brought his wife down in his arms. Many people cried when we moved away.

Mr Gordon's little girls visited Merrylegs for the last time.

Chapter 11   Earls Hall

The next morning, Joe came and he took Merrylegs away to Mr and Mrs Good's house.

John rode Ginger and took me to Earls Hall. It was a very big house with a lot of stables.

At the stables, John asked for Mr York, the boss of the drivers and grooms.

Mr York came and looked at us. 'Very good,' he said. 'They look very good, but horses are very different. You and I know that. What can you tell me about these two?'

'Well,' John said, 'there aren't any better horses than these in the country. But they are different. Black Beauty is never angry or afraid because nobody was unkind to him. When she came to us, Ginger was very unhappy. She often bit and kicked people. She changed at Birtwick Park. We were kind to her, and she's very good now. But people will have to be kind to her, or she will be bad again.'

'I'll remember that,' Mr York said. 'But there are a lot of drivers and grooms here. I can't watch all of them.'

Before they went out of the stable, John said, 'I have to tell you something. Not one of our horses at Birtwick Park used a bearing rein.'

'Well, they'll have to have a bearing rein here,' said Mr York.

'Oh,' said John.

'I don't like bearing reins, and Lord Westland is very kind to horses,' said Mr York. 'But Lady Westland – she's different. For her, everything has to look good. Her carriage horses have to have their heads up. So they have to have bearing reins.'

John spoke to us for the last time. Then he went, and we were very sad.

Lord Westland came to us the next day.

'Mr Gordon says they are good horses. I think he's right,' he said. 'But we can't have one black horse and one brown horse in front of a carriage in London. They can pull the carriage here in the country, and in London we can ride them.'

'They didn't have bearing reins at Mr Gordon's,' said Mr York. 'John told me.'

'Well,' Lord Westland said, 'put the bearing reins on, but only pull them up slowly. I'll speak to Lady Westland about it.'

In the afternoon a groom harnessed Ginger and me to a carriage, and then the groom took us to the front of the house. It was very big – bigger than Birtwick Park – but I didn't like it very much.

Lady Westland came out of the house. She was a tall woman. She walked round us and looked at us. She wasn't happy about something, but she didn't say anything. She got into the carriage. York put the whip lightly across my back, and we walked away.

The bearing rein wasn't bad that day. I always walked with my head up, and the rein didn't pull it up higher.

'Will Ginger be angry with the rein?' I thought.

But she was very good.

At the same time the next day we went to the door again.

Lady Westland came out and said: 'York, pull those horses' heads up.'

York got down and said, 'Please don't be angry with me, Lady Westland. These horses didn't use a bearing rein before now, and Lord Westland said, "Pull their heads up slowly." Do you want me to pull them higher now?'

'Yes!' she said.

York came to our heads and made the reins shorter.

When we climbed to higher ground, we wanted to put our heads down. We had to pull harder. The bearing rein stopped us, and our legs and backs had to work harder.

Ginger said to me, 'This isn't too bad. I won't say anything because they are kind to us here in every other way. I don't want to be bad, but bearing reins make me very angry.'

Chapter 12   Ginger is Angry

One day Lady Westland came out in very expensive clothes.

'Drive to Lady Richmond's house,' she said. But she didn't get into the carriage. 'When are you going to get those horses' heads up, York? Pull them up now!'

York came to me first. He pulled my head back with the bearing rein. It hurt me, and the bit cut my mouth.

Then he went to Ginger and he began to pull her head back. Ginger stood up on her back legs. Her ears went back, and her eyes were very angry. She began to kick and she tried to get away from the carriage. York and the groom couldn't stop her. Then she caught her legs in the harness and fell.

York sat on Ginger's head. He told the groom to get a knife and cut the harness. Lady Westland went into the house.

Nobody had time for me. I stood with my head back. The bit hurt my mouth.

Then York came and took away the bearing rein. He said, 'Why do we have to have these bearing reins? They make good horses bad, and they make our work harder. Lord Westland will be angry. But how can I say no to his wife when *he* never does?'

They never put Ginger into carriage harness again at Earls Hall. When she was well again after her fall, one of Lord Westland's younger sons took her for his riding horse.

I worked with the carriage, and for four months the bearing rein hurt me every day. I worked with Max, an older horse. He came from Lord Westland's stable in London.

'Why do they have to hurt us with bearing reins?' I asked him.

'They do things that way in London,' he said. 'In London the rich people's horses have to have their heads up. It made me ill, so I'm here now. I'll die soon.' He looked at me sadly. 'I hope you don't have to have the bearing rein every day. You'll die before you're old, too. People are very stupid.'

Chapter 13   Reuben Smith

In April, Lord and Lady Westland went to their London house and took York with them. Ginger and I and three or four other horses stayed at Earls Hall. Their sons and their sons' friends rode us.

Reuben Smith was the boss of the stables when York was away. He was a very good driver and a good groom. He liked horses, and horses liked him. Why was he only the groom? Why wasn't he a boss, too?

Max told me about him.

Reuben Smith sometimes got drunk. When he wasn't drunk, he was very good at his work. Everybody liked him. But when he was drunk, he wasn't the same man.

'I'll never get drunk again,' he told York. And so York wasn't afraid to leave the horses with Smith when he, York, was away.

◆

One day Lord Westland's younger son wanted to go to London.

'I'll get on the train at Hertford,' he told Smith. 'I want you to drive me there in my carriage. It can stay in the carriage-maker's in Hertford, because I want him to do some work on it. So bring a saddle and ride Black Beauty home to Earls Hall.'

Reuben Smith drove me to the carriage-maker's. Then he put the saddle on me and rode me to the White Horse hotel. There he asked the hotel groom for some good food for me.

'Have him ready for me at four o'clock,' he said.

He went to the hotel, and he met some men at the door. He came out again at five o'clock and told the hotel groom, 'I don't want to go before six. I'm with some old friends.'

The groom showed Smith one of my front shoes. 'That shoe will fall off soon,' he told Smith. 'Do you want me to do something about it?'

23

'No,' Smith said. 'It can't fall off before we get home.'

Those were strange words. Reuben Smith was usually careful about our shoes.

◆

He didn't come out at six o'clock – or at seven – or at eight. At nine o'clock he came out of the hotel with a lot of noise.

'You!' he shouted to the hotel groom. 'Bring me my horse!'

He was very angry with the groom – with everybody in the hotel. Why? I didn't know.

We weren't out of Hertford when he started to hit me with his whip. I went as fast as I could. He whipped me again.

It was dark, and I couldn't see very well. The road was very hard, and bad in places, and my shoe soon fell off.

But Smith was drunk and didn't see it. He didn't stop. He whipped me and shouted at me.

'Faster! Faster!' he cried.

The bad road cut into the foot without a shoe and hurt me.

And then I fell and threw Smith over my head on to the road. It was an accident.

He didn't move.

My legs hurt, but I stood up. I moved to the grass near the road and waited.

Chapter 14   An Accident

I waited there for a long time.

It was nearly midnight when I heard a horse's feet. Then I saw Max and a cart. They came down the road. I called to Max, and he answered me.

There were two grooms in the cart. They wanted to find Reuben. One of them jumped down from the cart and ran across to the man on the road.

I threw Smith over my head on to the road.

'It's Reuben, and he isn't moving,' he said. 'He - he's dead – cold and dead!'

The other groom got out of the cart and came to me. He used one of the cart's lights and looked at the bad cuts on my legs.

'Black Beauty fell!' he said. 'Black Beauty! What happened?'

He tried to take me to the cart, and I nearly fell again.

'Oh!' he said. 'Black Beauty's foot is bad, too. And look – there's no shoe! Why did Reuben ride a horse without a shoe?' He looked at the other groom, then said, 'He was drunk again!'

They put Reuben Smith into the cart, and then one of the grooms drove it to Earls Hall. The other man put something round my bad foot and we walked on the grass near the road.

The cuts on my legs and my bad foot hurt me, but after some time we got home.

◆

I was ill for weeks after that. The grooms did everything for me, but the cuts were very bad. When I could walk, they put me into a small field. My foot and my legs got better, but only after many weeks.

One day Lord Westland came to the field with York. He looked at my legs and was angry.

'We'll have to sell him,' he said. 'I'm very sad, because my friend Mr Gordon wanted Black Beauty to have a happy home here. But you'll have to send him to Hampstead.'

And so I went to Hampstead. One day each week they sell horses there.

A lot of people came and looked at me. The richer people went away when they saw my legs. Other people looked at my teeth and eyes, and they felt my legs. I had to walk for them. Some people's hands were hard and cold. To them I was only a horse for work. But some had kind hands, and they spoke to me kindly. They learnt more about me than the other people.

I liked one of the kind men. 'I can be happy with him,' I thought. 'He likes horses and he's kind to them.'

He was a small man, but he moved well and quickly, and his hands and his eyes were friendly.

'I'll give twenty-three pounds for this horse,' he said.

'Say twenty-five pounds, Mr Barker, and you can have him,' another man said. He sold the horses – it was his job.

'Twenty-four and no more,' the little man said.

'All right, I'll take twenty-four pounds,' said the other man. 'You've got a very good horse for your money, Jerry Barker. He'll be very good for cab work. You'll be very happy with him.'

The little man paid the money, then he took me away to a hotel. There was a saddle there for me. He gave me some very good food, and soon we were on our way to London.

Chapter 15   A London Cab Horse

There were a lot of horses and carriages and carts in the streets of the great city. It was night, but there were a lot of people on the roads and under the street lights.

There were streets and streets and streets. Then Jerry Barker called to somebody, 'Good night, George.'

Cabs waited in this street.

'Hello, Jerry!' came the answer. 'Have you got a good horse?'

'Yes, I think I have,' said Jerry.

'That's good. Good night.'

Soon we went up a little street, and then into a street with small houses. Opposite the houses there were stables and carriage-houses.

Jerry Barker stopped me at one of the little houses and called, 'Are you asleep?'

The door opened, and a young woman ran out, with a little girl and a boy.

'Hello! Hello! Hello!' they shouted happily.

My rider got down from the saddle.

'Hello!' he said. 'Now, Harry, open the stable door and I'll bring him inside.'

Soon we were all in the little stable. The woman had a light in her hand, and they looked at me.

'Is he good, Father?' asked the little girl.

'Yes, Dolly, as good as you are. Come and put a hand on him.' The little girl wasn't afraid.

'She's nice, and she's kind,' I thought. 'I'm going to love her.'

'I'll get him some nice food, Jerry,' the woman said.

'Yes, all right, Polly,' said Jerry.

Jerry loved his wife Polly, and his son and daughter. His son, Harry, was twelve years old. His daughter, Dolly, was eight. They loved him, too.

I never knew happier people. They didn't have a lot of money, because people didn't pay cab drivers very well. But they were always kind, and their love came out of the little house to the stable.

Jerry had a cab and two horses. The other horse was a big old white horse called Captain. That night, Captain told me about the work of a London cab horse.

'Only one horse pulls the cab,' he said. 'Mr Barker works for about sixteen hours each day from Monday to Saturday, but you and I will only work for eight hours. It's hard work, but Jerry is never unkind. A lot of cabmen are unkind, but not Jerry. You'll love him.'

And he was right.

Captain went out with the cab in the morning. Harry came into the stable after school and gave me food and water.

When Jerry came home for his dinner, Polly cleaned the cab. Harry helped Jerry to put the harness on me. They did it slowly because they didn't want to hurt me. There was no bearing rein, and the bit didn't hurt.

I was a London cab horse!

'I think he'll be happy with that,' Jerry said.

'What's his name?' Polly asked.

'The man in Hampstead didn't know,' said Jerry. 'We can call him Jack. We called our last horse Jack. What do you think, Polly?'

'Yes, all right,' said his wife. 'It's a good name.'

So Jack was my new name, and I started work.

I was a London cab horse!

Chapter 16   Jerry Barker

We went down the street and Jerry took me to a place behind the other cabs.

A big cabman came to me with other drivers. He was the oldest cabman there. He looked at me and put a hand on my back and legs.

'Yes,' he said, 'he's the best horse for you, Jerry Barker. You paid a lot of money for him, but you did well. He's a good horse, and he'll work hard for you.'

My work was very hard. The great city was a new place for me. I wasn't happy with the noise, the thousands of people, the horses, carriages and carts in the streets. But Jerry was a very good driver, and I wanted to make him happy. We did well.

Jerry never whipped me. Sometimes he put the whip on my back. That meant 'Go!' But he usually only moved the reins when he wanted me to go.

He and Harry groomed us well, and Captain and I always had good food, clean water and a clean stable. Harry was clever with stable work, and Polly and Dolly cleaned the cab in the mornings. They laughed and talked. They were a happy family.

One morning an old cab stopped next to ours. The horse was tired and thin. She was a brown horse and she looked at me with tired eyes.

'Black Beauty!' she said. 'Is it really you?'

'Ginger?' I said.

It *was* Ginger, but a very different Ginger. She told me her story. It was a very sad story.

'After a year at Earls Hall, they sold me,' said Ginger. 'But I was ill again and a horse-doctor came. Then a cabman bought me. He's got a lot of cabs and other cabmen use them. They pay him for them. These men aren't always careful or kind. They whip me and I have to work seven days a week. My life is hard. I'm very tired now. I'll be happy when I die.'

'I'm very sorry, Ginger,' I said.

I put my nose near hers. I think she was happy.

'You were a good friend,' she said.

Some weeks after this, a cart went past us. There was a dead horse in the back. It was a brown horse. I think it was Ginger.

Sometimes a person wanted Jerry to go fast in the cab. Often Jerry said, 'No. You want to go fast because you got up late. You have to start your journey early, and then you can get there more slowly.'

Sometimes people wanted to give him more money, but he did not go faster. But after I learnt to go through the London streets, we could go faster than most cabs.

'We'll go fast when somebody has to get somewhere quickly, Jack,' Jerry said to me.

We knew the quickest roads to the hospitals in London, and sometimes we made very quick journeys to them.

◆

One wet day we took a man to his hotel. After he went inside, a young woman spoke to Jerry. She had a little boy in her arms, and he was very ill.

'Where is St Thomas's Hospital?' she asked. 'Can you tell me? I'm from the country, and I don't know London. The doctor gave me a letter for St Thomas's Hospital. The hospital can help my son.'

'It's a long way, dear,' Jerry said. 'You can't walk there – not in this rain and with the boy in your arms. Get into the cab and I'll take you there.'

'Thank you,' she said, 'but I can't do that. I haven't got any money.'

'Did I say anything about money?' said Jerry. 'I'm a father, and I love children. I'll take you. Please get in.'

He helped her into the cab. She started to cry and he put a hand on her arm. Then he climbed up and took the reins. 'Let's go, Jack,' he said.

At the hospital Jerry helped the young woman through the big front door.

'I hope your little boy will soon be better,' he said.

'Thank you, thank you!' she said. 'You're a good, kind man.'

A woman came out of the hospital. She heard the words and looked at the 'good, kind man'.

'Jerry Barker!' she said. 'Is it you?'

Jerry smiled.

'Good,' the woman said. 'I can't find a cab today, in this weather, and I have to catch a train.'

'I'll take you,' said Jerry. 'Where do you want to go?'

'Paddington Station,' said the woman.

Chapter 17   More Changes

We took the woman to her train. Her name was Mrs Fowler and she knew Polly.

She asked a lot of questions about Polly and the two children. Then she said: 'And how are you, Jerry?'

'I'm all right now, Mrs Fowler,' said Jerry. 'But I was very ill last January. Polly doesn't like me to work in bad weather, but I *have* to work.'

'The cold weather is bad for you, Jerry,' said Mrs Fowler. 'You'll have to find different work. You can't be a cabman now.'

'I'd like to find work in the country,' said Jerry. 'Polly and the children like the country. But there isn't any work for me there.'

Before she caught her train, Mrs Fowler gave Jerry some money for the children.

'People in the country want good grooms and drivers,' she said. 'When you stop cab work, write to me.'

'Thank you,' said Jerry.

Every year Jerry was ill in the winter. But he didn't stop working, and he got iller and iller.

◆

One year, at Christmas, we took two men to a house, and they said to Jerry, 'Come here again at eleven o'clock.'

Jerry arrived at the right time, but the men didn't come out of the house. We waited and waited. It was a very cold night, and it snowed. Jerry put an old coat over me, then he tried to stay warm.

At one o'clock the two men came out of the house and got into the cab. They didn't say 'Sorry, we're late.' They didn't say anything.

When we arrived home, Jerry was ill. He couldn't work the next day, or the next day.

Polly cried about it. 'What can I do?' she said.

Then, one day, a letter came for Polly. It was from Mrs Fowler:

> *Dear Polly,*
>
> *My groom is leaving. He is going to do other work, and he wants to go next month. His wife will go with him, and she is my cook. Would you like to work for me? Jerry can be my*

groom and driver, and Harry can help him. You can be my
cook. There is a little house for you.

Please say you will come.

Mary Fowler

Jerry and Polly talked about it for two days. Then Polly wrote an answer. Her letter said, 'Yes, Jerry and I want to work for you, Mrs Fowler.'

I was very happy for them, but I was sad, too. I loved Jerry and Polly and the two children.

Some of Jerry's cabmen friends wanted to have me, but Jerry wanted me to have a better home.

'Jack's getting old,' he said, 'and the work of a cab horse is too hard.'

Before Jerry, Polly and the children went away, Jerry sold me to a farmer. His name was Mr Thoroughgood, and he knew about horses.

'I'll take Jack, your horse,' he said. 'I'll give him the best food and some weeks in a good field. Then I'll find a new home for him – with a good, kind person.'

Mr Thoroughgood took me away. It was April.

Jerry was ill after a bad time in January and February, but he came outside, with Polly and Harry and Dolly. He saw me for the last time.

'You'll be happy, dear old Jack,' Dolly said. 'I'll always remember you.'

Chapter 18   My Last Home

Mr Thoroughgood was very kind to me, and I had a very happy time on his farm.

'I feel younger,' I thought. But I wasn't a young horse now.

34

One day Mr Thoroughgood told the groom, 'We have to find a good home for Jack. He can work, I think, but not too hard.'

'The women at Rose Hall are looking for a good horse for their small carriage,' said the groom. 'They don't want a young horse. Young horses sometimes go too fast or run away.'

Mr Thoroughgood thought about that. Then he said, 'I'll take Jack to them. He's the horse for them. But will they be afraid when they see his legs? He hurt them somewhere. I'll take him to Rose Hall tomorrow. They can look at him.'

The next morning the groom cleaned my black coat, and then Mr Thoroughgood took me to Rose Hall.

The women were at home, but their driver was away. One of the women, Miss Ellen, liked me when she saw me.

'He has a very good, kind face,' she said. 'We'll soon love him.'

'He's very good,' Mr Thoroughgood said. 'But he fell down. Look at his legs.'

'Oh!' Miss Ellen's older sister said. She was Miss Bloomfield. 'Will he fall again?'

'I don't think he will,' the farmer said. 'He fell because he had a bad driver. Try him, Miss Bloomfield. Send your driver for him tomorrow. He can try Jack for a day or two.'

Miss Bloomfield was happier. 'You always sell us very good horses, Mr Thoroughgood,' she said. 'Thank you. We'll do that.'

The next morning a nice young man came to Mr Thoroughgood's farm. He looked at me and at my legs. Then he asked Mr Thoroughgood, 'Why are you selling this horse? I'm not happy with his legs.'

The farmer answered, 'I won't sell him before you try him. But I think you'll like him. Ride him, and then tell me. Say yes, and you can have him. Say no, and he can come home here.'

The groom took me to Rose Hall.

That evening he began to groom me. When my face was clean, he stopped. He looked at the white star.

'I remember Black Beauty's white star,' he said. 'He was a wonderful horse. And when I look at this horse's head, I remember Black Beauty's head too. Where is Black Beauty now? I'd like to know.'

When he came to my back, he stopped again. 'Here's some white on his back,' he said. 'That's strange. When I look at it, I remember the white on Black Beauty's back!'

The groom stood and looked at me. 'Black Beauty's star! Black Beauty's one white foot! The white on Black Beauty's back! It *is* Black Beauty!' he said. 'You are Black Beauty, my old friend! Beauty! Beauty! Do you know me? I was little Joe Green, and I nearly killed you.'

And he put his arms round my head.

I remembered a small boy, and this was a man. But it was Joe Green, and I was very happy. I put my nose up to him in a friendly way. And I never saw a happier man than him.

'This is wonderful, Beauty,' he said. 'We'll try to make you happy here.'

The next day Joe groomed me again and harnessed me to a very good small carriage. Miss Ellen wanted to try me, and Joe Green went with her. She was a good driver, and she was happy with me. Joe talked to her about me.

'He's Mr Gordon's old Black Beauty!' Joe said, happily. 'He's a wonderful horse!'

When we came back to Rose Hall, Miss Bloomfield came to the door.

'He's a beautiful horse,' she said. 'Is he a good horse, too?'

'Yes,' Miss Ellen said. 'Very, very good. His name is Black Beauty, and he was at Birtwick Park with Mr Gordon. Our dear friend Mrs Gordon loved him.'

'Beauty nearly died when he got the doctor for Mrs Gordon,' said Joe. And he told them the story.

'I'm going to write to Mrs Gordon. I'll tell her about Black Beauty,' said Miss Ellen. 'She'll be very happy.'

The next day they harnessed me to the carriage, and Miss Bloomfield drove in it. She said to Miss Ellen, 'We'll have the horse and we'll use his old name, Black Beauty.'

◆

It is a year later now. Joe is the best and kindest groom, and everybody loves me.

Miss Ellen says, 'We'll never sell you, Beauty.'

So I'll work happily for them. I'm not afraid of anything.

ACTIVITIES

Chapters 1–6

Before you read

1 Read the Introduction to the story. What will happen to Black Beauty? Will the story be happy or sad?

2 Find the words in *italics* in your dictionary. They are all in the story.

   a Which animals:
   – wear these? *bit collar harness reins saddle*
   – can you *ride*?
   – *bite*?

   b What do you find:
   – on a *farm*?
   – in a *field*?

   c Where do you usually find these?
   grass stable star

   d What do people do with these?
   carriage whip

   e What is the adjective from *beauty*?

   f What does a *groom* do?

   g You have to leave *soon*. Do you have to leave now or in a short time?

After you read

3 Who says these words? Who or what are they talking about?

   a 'Always do your work happily. Never bite or kick. Then he'll always be nice to you.'

   b 'Now he'll have to learn to work. He'll be a very good horse then.'

   c 'One day she bit James in the arm and hurt him.'

   d 'He is kind to the horses, and the horses like him.'

4 Work with another student.

   Student A: You are Mrs Gordon. Your husband is late from the city. Ask him about his journey.

   Student B: You are Mr Gordon. Tell your wife about your journey. Tell her about Black Beauty and the bridge.

Chapters 7–12

Before you read

5 Black Beauty is going to leave Birtwick Park. Why? What do you think?

After you read

6 Use the best question-word for these questions, then answer them.
What Who Why

   a ... starts a fire after he smokes in the stable?

   b ... isn't Black Beauty afraid of the fire when James takes him out of the stable?

   c ... does John give a letter to at three o'clock in the morning?

   d ... is Black Beauty ill after the ride from the doctor's house?

   e ... does John Manly want to do after he leaves Birtwick Park?

   f ... does a bearing rein do?

7 Is Black Beauty's life better or worse with the Westlands? Talk about it.

Chapters 13–18

Before you read

8 Will Black Beauty always work in the country? What do you think?

9 Find the words in *italics* in your dictionary:

   a Who or what pulls a *cart*?

   b Who drives a *cab* these days?

   c How do people feel when they are *drunk*?

After you read

10 Who or what:

   a gets drunk?

   b dies in an accident?

   c does Lord Westland sell?

   d lives with Jerry Barker?

   e dies after a hard life in the city streets?

   f does Jerry sell Black Beauty to?

   g does Joe Green see on Black Beauty's face?

11 Will Black Beauty be happy at Rose Hall? Why (not)?

Writing

12 How was Ginger's life different from Black Beauty's? How do you feel about Ginger's life?

13 Which person in the story do you like best? Which person do you not like? Why?

14 There was a lot of work for horses in Anna Sewell's time. What work do horses do in your country today?

15 Write a letter about *Black Beauty* to a friend. Did you enjoy it? Write about the story. What did you like? What did you not like?

Answers for the Activities in this book are published in our free resource packs for teachers, the Penguin Readers Factsheets, or available on a separate sheet. Please write to your local Pearson Education office or to: Marketing Department, Penguin Longman Publishing, 5 Bentinck Street, London W1M 5RN.